One Lone Friend

A Novel in Three Movements
by

Bill Webb

Book One of The Lopeha Adventures

Look for Book II of the Lopeha Adventures:

Rushing Waters
by Bill Webb

To be published late 2019

Go to:

www.billwebbmusic.com

for:

- The companion album, "One Lone Friend" to hear the music from the book,

- The Lopeha Adventure novel updates,

- All of Bill Webb's music/videos/podcasts,

- Native American Flute Music Podcasts,

- Dozens of peaceful music videos,

- The Bill Webb Blog

- Also, facebook.com/NativeAmericanFlute

- and...@billwebbmusic on Twitter

One Lone Friend

Copyright 2018

William G. Webb

Published by Bill Webb Music: www.billwebbmusic.com

Cover Art by Brian Rott: www.quasimondo.org

1st Edition 2018

2nd Edition July 2019

ISBN 978-1-7329396-3-9
Library of Congress Control Number:2019909517

Book I of the Lopeha Adventures Series

featuring John Whitlock and Terry Silverman

All characters and their stories are fictitious and in no way represent real persons living or otherwise. Although historical and current events references are made, the locations and names of all places and specific events are fictitious.

Lopeha means "love, peace and harmony".

"The voice that is beckoning us to view ourselves,
is the one that reveals man's soul to himself."

Anonymous

Caution: Reading of this book may be

hazardous

to your concepts of reality.

Thank you, Marsha for being my grammar guru

Table of Contents

Prelude: The Guides..6

First Movement: The Preparation......................35
Chapter One: John...................................36
Chapter Two: Terry...................................41
Chapter Three: John.................................46
Chapter Four: Terry..................................51
Chapter Five: John...................................60
Chapter Six: Terry....................................67
Chapter Seven: John.................................74
Chapter Eight: Terry.................................82

First Interlude: The Prospector.........................94

Second Movement: Into Action........................105
Chapter One: Terry's Serenity.......................106
Chapter Two: John's First Awakening.............111
Chapter Three: The Reunion.........................123
Chapter Four: Sadoval the Navajo.................136
Chapter Five: The Plan..............................146
Chapter Six: Sadoval at the Diner..................155
Chapter Seven: John's Second Awakening.....167
Chapter Eight: John and Terry Regroup.........177

Second Interlude: The Uranium King..............187

Third Movement: The Path of Home................200
Chapter One: The Uranium Mine....................201
Chapter Two: Sadoval's Transition.................220
Chapter Three: John's Light...........................231
Chapter Four: The Return..............................244

Postlude: The Guides II..................................253

Notes and Links..265

Prelude:

The Guides

Johnny Whitlock was born into a suburban working-class family that became wealthy during his childhood. His parents never grew up, which he never knew, and he was expected to act grown up at a very young age. Johnny felt abandoned by his Dad and abused by his Mom. Dad put work before family, and self-indulgence before family needs, a combination that kept Dad away most of the time. Mom stayed at home trying hard to accomplish those household duties for which she had no experience and few skills. Frustrated and angry at her husband's carousing and neglect, she regularly vented her anger upon Johnny who was often afraid to come home not knowing if he would be greeted by another of his Mom's rages.

Johnny's grandfather, George Whitlock, died when Johnny was six leaving one small corner grocery store in the decaying ghetto of their lovely city of Miswalkie to his only son. Convenience stores were a new and fast-growing business in the early 1970's, and Grandpa George also left a business plan, newly completed and ready for implementation, to turn Whitlock's Grocery into a franchised chain: Whitlock's Grab 'n Go, a symbol of success that became Johnny's bane. It took Dad away, made Mom even more angry and Johnny grew up with a pining for emotional comfort, no stable or present role models for getting it, nor any ability to give it out to others.

Johnny had a recurring dream during his grade school days that Dad had promised to come home from work early in the day and take him swimming. Johnny would be waiting in the back yard in the warm sunshine basking in the excitement of a day at the beach with Dad. The dream began with the sun rising in the sky filling the morning with warmth and hope. Perfect swimming weather. The hours passed with no Dad.   The sun moved across the sky and Johnny got scared. *Dad promised he would come. There's still time. If Dad would come home now, we could still go.* His fear grew, but he would gauge the position of the sun and reassert his hope by rationalizing that, at any moment, Dad would drive up, scoop him into his arms and they would be off to the beach. The day dragged on until despair defeated hope as Johnny realized Dad would never come.   That beautiful day at the beach with Dad sank into darkness along with the sun. The most impactful part of the dream was seeing himself lying on the backyard hammock in the gloomy dusk staring at a gray overcast sky having intense feelings of despair and abandonment.

The dream always ended with his Mom's voice screaming a long string of the worst swear words he had ever heard. Johnny would wake up sobbing, alone in the darkness in his empty room longing for something to comfort his despair.   As an adult, Johnny realized that this dream epitomized his relationship with both parents: abandonment by Dad, condemnation by Mom. What was too painful to think about when he was awake, came forth from his subconscious in his dreams. Fear of abandonment, rejection, loneliness and despair became the driving forces in his life, forces that led him to selfish overindulgence in human pleasures and blinded him to his own needs and the needs of others. But hope did not stay defeated. Johnny was born with a precious and loving heart that would come to mean joy, peace and happiness for himself and many others. His life became a roller coaster ride that eventually crashed into the wall at the end of the track jolting him into a new dimension.

His Mom offered little comfort as she was incapable of being emotionally supportive. She was angry, frustrated and unfulfilled in her marriage, and had never come to terms with the childhood abuse she suffered at the hands of her own alcoholic Father. Johnny was often the innocent target of her anger. She would scream and cuss at him for the smallest infractions often slapping him repeatedly until he fell to the floor. He attempted to protect himself by trying hard to please his mom, to be perfect for her so she would not get angry and hurt him. But no matter what he did, he could not seem to please her. He developed guilt feelings without behaving any worse than a normal boy. He became gun shy and afraid around his Mom. He never knew what to expect as her behavior was so unpredictable. One minute she would act kind and loving, and the next she would fly into a rage. Home was not a safe place and Johnny needed a way out.

Johnny was too naïve to devise schemes to avoid his Mom's rages, and too afraid to confront her. Besides, he was born with a loving heart that commonly overrode retaliatory behavior. That loving heart motivated him to write cute little poems to his Mom, or he would invent little word games and get her to play them in her calmer moments. He wrote a poem to her on Mother's Day when he was ten that expressed his heart's deepest desire for his Mom to be relieved of all her grief and emotional pain:

It's Mother's Day and all is well,
I'm running down the street pall mall;
To give you this very special letter,
I hope it will make you feel better.

This loving heart, in spite of being beaten down and all but destroyed, became the tiny spark that would fuel a new glorious life, after a tragic experience as an adult brought him to his knees and gave him the willingness to listen to his heart and learn to follow the commands of its love.

With Dad gone most of the time, and Mom wrapped up in her own internal struggles, little Johnny was often left to discover the world and its dark ways on his own. He accepted this state of affairs because it gave him lots of time away from his raging Mom and distracted him from feeling that intense longing for the closer relationship with his Dad he could not have. This lack of mature role models coupled with his short slight frame and cute baby-faced innocence made it difficult for him to assert himself and establish a credible presence especially among his peers. He was often targeted by bullies and more often ignored by his classmates. But Johnny was clever, almost brilliant. He had a way of figuring things out for himself which helped him develop some survival skills in lieu of parental direction. For example, with no lessons on how to cross the busy street in front of his house at age six, he was left to do so every day to school and Sundays to church. He had learned about traffic safety in school and was alert and attentive when walking to school. He prided himself on his self-sufficiency but seldom received accolades for it.

He learned more at school from teachers and students than he did from his parents on how to cope with life, good and bad. Because school felt much safer than home, he relaxed there and felt freer to use his mind and develop new skills. At home it was a struggle for emotional survival.

The more nurturing school environment naturally brought out Johnny's inherent ability to be a high achiever. A high IQ and cleverness also made him an outstanding grade school student. He almost always got 'A's' except in fifth grade where the teacher, a very crabby lady that reminded him of his Mom, made him feel almost as unsafe in the classroom as at home and it affected his concentration and motivation to learn.

From age six on, after school and Saturday morning chores, Johnny went off on his own for the rest of the day playing and adventuring throughout the growing neighborhood of cookie cutter houses, empty fields, open creeks and housing construction. Here he could feel free to express himself as he wished. His adventures were harmless enough, but very important to his survival, for within them he created his own private safe place. He was given a twenty-inch bicycle at age seven which expanded his adventure land to the entire suburb and within weeks he was riding anywhere he wanted through the city: the toy store, school, the drug store to buy comic books, church, or just plain discovery rides. His weekly chores included sweeping out the basement, mowing the lawn or shoveling snow, sweeping the driveway and cleaning his room. His Dad made it clear that there were no free rides in this world, and that Johnny's weekly allowance was compensation for work done. Each year his wages increased along with his duties, administered by Dad the same way he ran his business. Money became the sign of praise and approval from his Dad rather than nurturing and intimacy. Dad became obsessed with growing the new chain of stores, and alcohol, gambling and sex addictions made him emotionally incapable of expressing love to his family which fueled Johnny's alienation and loneliness and led him down his own path of alcoholism and despair.

Seven was Johnny's magic number. On July 7, 1977, Johnny turned seven and three things happened that would be the harbingers of events that would eventually transform him into something more amazing than anything he could have ever imagined.

First, the most influential relationship of his childhood began with Terry Silverman. Johnny saw him walking on the other side of the street carrying a grocery bag from 'The Beer Depot' - the "go to" place for Mom's to send their kids for those last minute staples - bread and milk. This skinny, tall fair haired boy called out, "Hey, do you want to be my best

13

friend?" and Johnny ran across the street to take his place. There were no other introductions. It was as if the two boys already knew each other intimately and needed no words. They shared a common bond of feeling odd, different, rejected and emotionally neglected. Terry's Dad was an abusive alcoholic, especially toward Terry's sisters. But Johnny knew none of this, nor did he ever share with Terry anything about his own parents, at least not until Terry saw it for himself. They had the radar sense of children of abusive or alcoholic families. They could intuitively detect one of their own kind and be drawn into a relationship. But in their young minds, they knew little of the nature of this bond. They simply felt it and acted upon it naturally and spontaneously. They needed each other to survive.

Terry had been born prematurely, almost albino with no eyebrows or hair. He was thin and small boned, with a large head which Johnny always felt needed to be large to hold his big brain because Terry was so smart. He always got straight 'A's' without hardly ever studying. Terry's breast-bone stuck out abnormally to the point that he laughingly called himself 'chicken-breast', but only to Johnny. Johnny liked the oddness of Terry's big head and chicken-breast. It made him feel comfortable because, although Johnny had no unusual features himself, and was actually quite good-looking, he felt like a freak from the circus, so he never ever made fun of Terry's looks.   In fact, Johnny always thought that Terry was the handsome one.   Besides his odd features, Terry was healthy and strong and able to carry on like any able-bodied boy.

Now Johnny had a fellow explorer for after school and Saturday adventures.   This suited Terry well for it was crowded at his home.   He had three sisters and two brothers in a two-bedroom house with an attic.   The girls shared the second story bedroom and the boys crowded into the third story attic that Dad had fashioned into a rudimentary bedroom. Johnny, on the other hand, had his own bedroom and even a private bathroom so Terry spent almost every Saturday night sleeping over at Johnny's house away from his own chaos. They would play army in the fields and muddy construction sites, build plastic models of ships, planes and cars in Johnny's room, ride their bicycles to undiscovered lands in nearby neighborhoods and take trips to the toy stores at the malls and neighborhood shopping centers.   Their adventures usually included playing army with an imaginary platoon of men. They would each find a stick or piece of wood that felt like a machine gun and crawl up mounds of dirt to prepare for attack. The enemy always killed off the entire platoon except for the two brave young warriors who would in turn single-handedly defeat the entire insurgency on their own. It was on these adventures that the two friends felt powerful, even invincible, a very necessary respite from the attacks they suffered at home from their parents, before which they were helpless.

Yelling and screaming from Johnny's Mom was the primary source of chaos at Johnny's house, and this was tolerable for Terry because it was never directed at him and was a lot better than at his own home. Her tirades of cussing would sometimes occur when Terry was present. She would be in the kitchen slapping Johnny's arms and legs as he held them up to protect himself while Terry faded into the living room seemingly ignored and waited it out. What he did not know was that Johnny was acutely aware that Terry could hear what was happening and was more than embarrassed. He was completely ashamed. His Mom was a small woman, but to little Johnny, who was always small for his age, it felt like he was being attacked by a giant. He could count on being yelled at for muddy shoes, a dirty face or being late for lunch and it did not seem to matter if Johnny was alone or with Terry. She would lay down an explicative with every blow. 'Take that you little bastard!' and 'How - dare - you - track - mud - on - my - kitchen - floor - you god - dam - ass - hole!' When he got the 'Go to your room!' command, Johnny would jump up and run through the living room Terry at his heels, up the stairs into his bedroom, red with rage, tears streaming down his face, and call his Mom all the same swear words she had just used on him. Terry would literally roll on the floor with laughter, laughing harder with each explicative. Cuss words were not allowed in Terry's home, so he overreacted with hysterical laughter to cover up his own fear and pain. It was a release valve for both of them, spontaneous survival therapy that bonded the boys much like prisoners of war, which may explain how well the boys took to playing army and being the last desperate soldiers to survive the enemy.

Johnny found some other moments of respite from Mom's daily beatings and Dad's absence in his imaginative playtime adventures with Terry. But Terry was not always available, and the emotional neglect and abuse from his parents made him desperately needy. He needed emotional satisfaction every minute of every day. His fears demanded it. Later in his teens, without Terry, he found alcohol, sex and the rock band. The moments of comfort they provided were soon replaced by one disaster after another until he hit the bottom of his self-made pit of alcoholism, and almost lost everything meaningful in his life.

The second life changing thing happened in the fall of Johnny's seventh year when he came home from school to find a brand-new mahogany piano in the living room.

His heart jumped with excitement. "Can I play it!?" he asked his Mom. "I tell you what," Mom replied, "how about you and me both take piano lessons. Would you like that, Sunny Boy?" She always called him 'Sunny Boy' when she was happy, and this was one of those remarkable moments when she acted like the perfect loving Mom.

So, Johnny took lessons and was required to practice a half hour every day, but he often practiced for over an hour a day. He would focus all his concentration on learning his lessons. When he was working on a new piece of music, he would stay with it until he could play it perfectly. He would sometimes get frustrated when he made the same mistake over and over and pound his fist on the piano in anger. His Mom would yell from the kitchen, "You stupid idiot. You're gonna break the damn piano!" and he would answer by trying to play it again and again. Of course, he would stop sooner or later because Terry was coming over and they had mountains to climb, deserts to cross and enemies to defeat.

On the piano, he devoted his heart to learning new songs. It stilled his unsettled emotions and made him forget about his parents if only for a little while. Adventures with Terry had much the same effect as adventures in music, but with Terry he had much needed companionship. With the piano, he was alone. Music became more than a comfort; it boosted his self-esteem and it became an expression of his innermost self. With Terry, he had a living breathing flesh and blood person, and home troubles would disappear in his presence. With the piano, he had a secret friend, one over which he had supreme control, and he clung to his music like the drowning cling to life vests.

So, the good side of Johnny's grade school years consisted of school, which he enjoyed, adventures with Terry, and a fast-growing ability to play the piano and eventually create his own music. The bad side was waiting for his Dad, a mostly fruitless endeavor, and either placating his Mom or being abused by her.

But there was one more thing Johnny had going for him, something tiny and subtle, like a quiet voice calling from a distance place, beckoning him toward something he could not yet understand, but which would eventually more than make up for all the hurts of his family life.

This was the third thing that happened to Johnny in the magical sevens of his childhood. In that summer of 1977, he had an experience so fleeting some may say it was too insignificant to be noteworthy. Yet it would later grow into the most powerful thing in his life.

It was summer vacation on a Saturday morning and Johnny was painfully going about his weekly chore of sweeping the cold gray basement floor. He was depressed and would rather have been outside playing army with Terry, going on a bicycle adventure or exploring the open creek bed in the nearby field. The dusty dimness was lit only by the sunlight coming through the three small rectangular window wells at the top of the cement block basement walls. A sunbeam slanting through the window illuminated millions of dust particles, aroused from their week long sleep by his broom, and turned them into shimmering diamonds. He stood still and watched the tiny sparkles swirl in the sunlight and disappear beyond its borders. The three charcoal gray furnaces, lined up near the back wall of the basement, loomed in the silence like dependable steady thoughts waiting quietly to be brought forth to dissolve the cacophony of fears and worries that shouted in his mind. For a moment his mind quieted and he felt a completely alien sensation of safety and comfort. At that moment, a blurry figure appeared to the side of his line of sight and disappeared behind the furnaces. He thought he heard an old man laughing. His heart jumped with fear and excitement. He jerked his head toward it and saw nothing. He looked away hoping and fearing to catch another glimpse from the corner of his eye. He saw nothing but felt a strong presence of something beautiful and foreboding. He moved slowly and quietly to the furnaces and quickly peeked behind them. He saw nothing as his heart pounded against his ears. He crept behind the furnaces, walked to the last one and jerked his head around it to see - nothing. Only emptiness. Then heard a voice in his head saying, "Hey, Johnny." It did not seem to come from his thoughts. It was like someone had planted a radio in his brain and was broadcasting to him. He heard, "Hey, Johnny," again. The voice was comforting, warm, inviting. He felt his heart being drawn to it. It lit a tiny spark of hope inside that something exciting was to come, like there was some promised land to which he was being called to do something very important. Then the moment was over. The voice and the ghostly figure were gone. His loneliness and fear crept back in and he moped back to where he had left off and continued sweeping in silent mourning of the loss of an elusive feeling of he knew not what, but which would later become the foundation for a whole new life.

Whitlock's Grab 'n Go prospered into a large regional chain of stores and Dad got rich. So, when Johnny was twelve and ready to enter seventh grade, they moved away to the land of the rich, a portentous subdivision just north of where all the landed gentry of Miswalkie lived, and where newbies like themselves could feel a little more important. It was a different world, far away from Terry and all their adventures. Adolescence is a time of great change, a time of questioning what has been important and trying out new things. It is a time of insecurity that requires guidance, support and love to traverse effectively. Given Johnny's turbulent home life and extreme emotional insecurity, he had few tools to cope with adolescence much less with a complete change in social structure, a new school and an abrupt move upward. In fact, it was unbearable.

He was placed in the local 'school for rich kids' by his Dad who told him, "You are going to get the education I never got." He did not want to go to this new school, it was more like a jail sentence, and he did not understand these new people at all. They were nothing like what he was used to. Shoes, clothing and hairstyles were all different. They even talked differently and used expressions he had never heard. He adjusted poorly to the culture shock of jumping so far and so quickly in the caste system - from public school to college preparatory. These new kids did not accept him from the start.

On his first day in school, a kid dressed like all the others, stopped in his tracks in the hallway and stared at Johnny's very different shoes, shirt and hair style. He shouted up and down the hall, "Look at the Cowboy! Hey everybody, look at the cowboy!" It was not the cowboy reference that bothered him, it was the sarcasm with which he spoke. Johnny became acutely aware of how different he looked. They were from rich families who had been wealthy for generations and owned much of Miswalkie and they looked and acted it to the hilt, lording it over little Johnny low-life. Johnny was from the working-class suburbs. His Dad was uneducated, and they made fun of him and his convenience stores that catered to the 'poor people'. They were disgusting, dirty places in the wrong parts of town that no respectable person would ever enter.

Johnny did not have the emotional stamina to stand up for himself. He had no support from home as his parents' emotional maturity was not much further along than his own. He went from loud to soft and became an introvert and underachiever, leaving behind the excited and enthusiastic boy adventurer and public school 'A' student and becoming the outcast with no personality who could not even make honor roll. He spent all of his time trying to protect himself from the ridicule and snobbery of these new peers instead of asserting his place among them. He was unable to find a boy to replace his childhood best friend.

Grades, dating, friendships, sports all became a struggle as he wallowed in loneliness and depression. Unable to conjure up any meaningful new friendships, he'd lie in bed listening to motivational LPs from his parents' library of Dale Carnegie and Norman Vincent Peale getting pumped up with hope and courage that tomorrow morning would be different; that he'd be storming the school bristling with confidence, 'acing' his classes, captaining the baseball team and asking that cheerleader Valerie Kames out on a date. Yet every morning he would wake up with all confidence lost, drag himself out of bed and trudge to school feeling like worm slime knowing he could never walk shoulder to shoulder with the Jim Rieslings with their class presidencies and captaincies and cheerleader girlfriends. Valerie never even noticed him.

Johnny retreated into a cocoon of fear, fear that weaved its sinewy tendrils into every aspect of his life. Transplanted from his working-class neighborhood of small cookie-cutter houses, tiny front lawns, sidewalks and curbs to this nouveaux riche suburb of four pillar houses atop hills overlooking fields and woods and lakes should have been a blessing but, separated from Terry, his inherent emotional insecurity manifested as a large hulking fear which began to move him in dark and foreboding directions. His parents became less available than ever as Dad took on yet another business, which turned out to be a great excuse to be gone most of the time, including overnights: a pretty sad state of affairs considering the businesses were right there in Miswalkie. Dad's neglect of Mom turned her into a ghostly figure sitting alone by the front window awaiting his arrival for dinner, often delayed or cancelled without even a phone call.

By age fourteen, 'Johnny' became 'John' in an attempt to establish himself as mature. He had learned to avoid his Mom and thicken the wall of emotional protection around him into an almost impenetrable barrier to making friends. He would take long walks alone through the swampy woods, and around the centerpiece of his wannabe subdivision, a murky lake without a name fed by overflow from the polluted Miswalkie River. He had a peculiar fascination for the swamp as its ambience was dark and cold with a foreboding that was similar to his soul and sent shivers down his spine. Its murky deep woods center was said to have never been explored which provided the challenge and diversion his lonely desperate soul needed.

One cold overcast autumn Saturday, John found himself hopping from tree root to tree trunk toward the center of the swamp. After a few minutes, he looked up into the sunless sky and realized he had lost his sense of direction. He glanced back at the maze of trees towering above the brackish water on their little mounds of soft moss. They all looked alike. Panic set in as he searched wildly for something familiar, his heart beating rapidly, his stomach filled with fear.

He remembered moss grew on the north side of trees, but all the tree trunks appeared to be covered in moss on all sides. Gloomy hangings of god knows what surrounded him and seemed to get thicker. On the move again, he jumped from mound to mound, the mounds getting smaller and the gaps between them wider. He leaped too wide an expanse and slipped sinking into muck up to his knees. He tried to pull his legs up spasmodically grasping the air with his arms. His feet were completely stuck and the more he struggled the deeper he seemed to go.

The water rose above his knees and the once brave adventurer began to scream in panic. In the flash of a moment, he felt a great pressure on his shoulders as if something or someone was trying to push him down. Terror shot through his body like a shiver of iced lightening and he screamed, "No! No! No!" In that same instant he felt light as a feather and with renewed energy gave his leg a big hoist. It broke loose and he stepped onto the soft moist ground almost effortlessly.

He turned around in time to see an indefinable blur of some sort whisk away through the swamp. He heard the faint sound of something like an old man chuckling. A hot prickly chill went up through the top of his head as he turned away with mixed feelings of fear and safety and peered through the trees. His eyes immediately fell on a yellow road sign in a clearing up ahead as he heard an almost familiar voice inside his mind say, "Hey, Johnny."

He never returned to that swamp. Even in winter when it and the lake froze over, he only skated near the edge. But he often wondered whether he had escaped an attempt by something evil to do him in, or if the pressure he felt pushing him down was some kind of angel that motivated him to gain his freedom.

The first three years in the new school brought out a hundred forms of fear in Johnny. He was afraid of his classmates and their verbal attacks. He was afraid of not fitting in and in his emotional withdrawal he became afraid of taking any action in front of anyone for fear of ridicule and punishment. He fell into a depressive slump, quit piano lessons, and, outside of school, became a loner. It was safer alone. Loneliness was his dominant emotion. He felt alone even in a crowd at school and was unable to do well in his studies, athletics and social life. School that had always been a respite from the terror of home life was now an even bigger terror. Having no friends, only mockers left him lonely and his ambition was drowned by his depression. He had nowhere to turn, no escape from this internal pain and struggle.

But the spark in his heart would not let him just roll over and play dead for long. He began sitting at the piano and making up melodies. He found some old blues music and liked the beat so much, he invented his own blues songs. He heard someone at school talking to a teacher about a jazz artist, so after school he went to the dusty old grand piano in the back stage of the school auditorium and made up his own jazz. It felt exciting. He loved it, and he hoped others would hear how good it was and come running in from the hallway to see what extraordinary musician was performing such incredible music. But no one came. They had all gone home and he knew it. They probably would have ridiculed him anyway, so he definitely did not have the courage to ask anyone to come in and listen.

In ninth grade John braved going on that first date, conspired by the Moms after meeting at a parent social night and discovering they had a perfect match for their children. This he always remembered as the Homecoming disaster with Beth Wilson - an Amazonian girl almost a foot taller with a reputation for doing crazy things like smashing the window while playing airplane in the boy's room and cutting her hand, which she just happened to do on their date during the Homecoming dance. There was the scream from the boys' room, blood everywhere, EMT's scurrying about and carrying her out on a stretcher, and the worst part, everyone at the dance standing there with smirks on their faces and ridicule in their eyes. He had been trying hard enough not to be noticed at the dance, and now everyone was staring at him. Beth was not seriously hurt and had gone quite cheerfully to the ambulance. But he was left behind to spend the rest of the dance in quiet humiliation alone in the corner of the room.

This experience deepened his terror of females that began with his raging Mother, so much so that Jim Riesling, the class president, took pity on him, if only briefly. Jim took him aside and told him he could do better. He should start with one of the shorter, less homely and slightly less unpopular girls and work his way up. His self-esteem was much too low to go asking any more girls out, and Jim did not seem to care enough to help out with more than advice, so he dipped into the pool of public school seventh graders in his neighborhood where his lack of reputation was unknown, and he could make some headway in establishing an identity of importance. It was there he discovered the great temporary fixes that would consume the next two decades of his life: Rock, romance and whiskey.

By the summer before tenth grade a few of the soon to be public school eighth graders formed a rock band and asked John, the sophisticated older boy that played the piano, to play keyboard with them. John's Dad, in an earnest attempt to assuage his own underlying guilt for never being around, bought him a new portable keyboard and John was on his throne as the new King of Rock. They practiced for a month in the drummer's basement which just happened to be right next door to a very cute red head who was a friend of the guitar player. Andrea was almost thirteen, but you might have guessed she was sixteen. She had long thick deep auburn hair that flowed over freckled ivory shoulders onto very full breasts exposed mightily by the tank tops she wore to every practice. Her ivory face was lightly freckled which gave her an innocent, childlike look, but her well defined cheekbones expressed maturity. She would sit across from him during practice and shoot sparkling glances through bright blue eyes that sent tingles from his stomach to his groin. He had mixed feelings of fear of girls and shame for being attracted to someone two years younger (a huge gap when you're in ninth grade) which kept him from doing anything more than offering a quick smile now and then and burying his attention in the keyboard. But, when she sat on his lap after his band won first place in a local contest, he gave in to the tingling and felt like his whole world had turned into a blissful fairy tale of love and adventure. The ecstasy of sex became his new way out.

The band and the girl were his saving graces. He played music on stage and imagined himself a rock star, cementing himself to her between gigs. It became a necessary relief from his fear and depression which were now temporarily buried in this new array of admiration, accolades and romance. In between he got drunk. The band was a close substitute for a best friend but was too unpredictable to fulfill all his needs for attention and confidence building. Members would come and go, and he was never quite certain how they would behave. The rendezvous with Andrea were pure bliss. Their sex was an excellent temporary antidote to his fear and depression. He would do anything to see her. Sneaking out of his window at night and walking two miles through a golf course and across a rushing waterfall on the Miswalkie River to have sex with her, often falling asleep until dawn and then rushing back home to find his Dad having coffee by the patio door right below his bedroom window. He came up with excuses like, "I was out practicing my cross-country running," or, "I took the dog for a walk." Hungover Dad never said a word, but he never knew if Dad was just out of it and didn't comprehend what he was saying, or if he believed him or not. It was worth all the trouble, though. Those midnight encounters were islands of serenity in the midst of emotional chaos.

When he wasn't performing, he needed Andrea. When he wasn't with her, he needed to perform. But there was a lot of time in between to help him develop his role as a despondent victim of he didn't know what, layered over bitterness layered over deep-set resentment against *them* layered over feelings that were the opposite of feeling loved until it was too hideous to feel at all. Getting drunk temporarily kept those feelings at bay, burying them deeper and deeper until, in his early thirties, alcohol became the fuel that caused the explosions that woke him up to a new life.

He asked Andrea to marry him two years out of high school. She said yes, then no, then declared she was a lesbian. This rejection pierced his emotional barrier and a flood of excruciating feelings spewed forth. To escape at least some of the pain, he quickly found a daily relationship with marijuana, pizza and beer. After three months, the smoke cleared and he was able to convince another one of those former public school seventh graders to marry him. Jane Shepherd, a very pretty girl with a slender figure, small breasts and long straight deliciously thick brown hair. They found their love in the back seat of his Toyota in the early morning hours after a Saturday night gig.

They both got drunk and threw up on their honeymoon campout and began their adult life as children. Jane wanted a child, but John would not even consider it. His aversion to parenthood came from the negative role models his parents presented and from the fact that he had not yet grown up himself. He still craved the attention of a child, loving attention that every child naturally seeks but which he never received. Deep inside, he was afraid to bring anyone into a world that was so frightening and dangerous. Even deeper in his subconscious, he was afraid of himself and becoming just like his parents. Life became nightmarish. The gigs on weekend nights in beer bars were often followed by drunken back seat trysts. During the days, hungover and shame ridden, he attempted to build a recording business with one of his colleagues - a guitar player angrier than he. His drinking had escalated to the point where he would start his day by telling his wife he had a meeting with his partner, telling his partner he was going out to try and scout some new business, and then going to the liquor store and getting a fifth of Jack Daniels and spending the entire day drunk wandering around Miswalkie. Back seat sex after gigs sometimes developed into a relationship on the side where he kept his marriage a secret from 'her' and 'her' a secret from Jane. The juggling of lies to his wife, his partner, and to himself was wearing him thin. He had to get away or he would explode. He felt he had messed his life up so badly it could never be fixed. By this time, all he seemed to know how to do was drink booze. He drank every day, and if there was no gig to play that night, he would often go into an alcohol blackout and not remember where he went or what he did.

So, in the biggest drunken binge of his life, he told off his partner, screamed at his wife, packed a bag and drove west. His wife divorced him, his business partner condemned him and John...well, he tried very hard to stay sober and make a new life in Austin, Texas.

First Movement:

The Preparation

Chapter One: John

John Whitlock came barreling into the driveway and screeched to a halt nearly running over the tricycle with his gray 1989 Chevy Cavalier. *Damn that girl, she should know better at her age.* Three-year old Sarah came around from the side of the house with arms outstretched, her blonde curls bouncing as she ran.

"Daddy, Daddy!" she cried out.

"I told you never to leave your trike in the driveway! Now go put it up this instant!" He ignored her plea for a hug and the three-year-old sulked over to the trike and wheeled it to its proper place on the patio. John looked at his twelve-year-old pile of junk car and felt depressed. *All this time and what do I have to show for it.* The thought gloomed in his mind. He noticed his wife, Judith, arms crossed, glaring through the screen door of their small two-bedroom ranch house and felt a pang of guilt. He quickly changed his attitude.

"I'm sorry, honey," he said to Sarah who gave him a dry-eyed whimper and reached out her arms once again. He scooped her up and carried her toward the house.

"Uh, hi Jude," he said sheepishly with all the smile he could force as he tried hard to suppress his residual anger.

"John, she's only *three*," Judith reprimanded with a concerned tone.

"Hey, look. When *I* was three there were no excuses. You did what you were supposed to or you got it!" His anger resurfaced and he geared up for the evening argument. She was ready for him.

"Now look, John, I will *not* have you treating our daughter that way. She is just a little girl. You expect too much from her."

"Too much! Too much!" He put Sarah down firmly on the front stoop. "You're too much, ya know that! Get off my back!" John's face was red and his hands were visibly shaking. He looked anxiously past Judith into the living room, his instincts more than his logic drawing him toward that bottle of brandy in the wet bar.

"I just want you to be a little more civil toward her." She knew his buttons and couldn't help but push them.

"Civil! I'm the most civil guy in the world! Ask anybody at work. They'll tell you! You're the only one in the world who doesn't know it! I'm civil! I'm nice! I just expect people to put things back where they belong!"

"Yeah, you're civil all right. Just look at you yelling out here where all the neighbors can hear!"

"Let 'em hear. They can hear how my own family doesn't appreciate me. How nobody listens to me! How I'm not even welcome in my own home!" He was screaming now,** and Judith knew she had pushed too far. She softened her voice.

"John. Come into the house. Supper's almost ready." She stepped aside and he barged through the door, went straight to the liquor cabinet and filled a six-ounce glass with whiskey.

"Oh, John. Not tonight. I was hoping we could have a nice family dinner."

"Look, I've been working my ass off all week long. All week long!"

"What do you think I've been doing around here, sunbathing and eating chocolates! Now put down that drink and be civil for once!"

"There you go with that civil thing again. Look at *you*, you're no Mary Tyler Moore!"

"What's *that* supposed to mean."

"You know very well what it means. It means I'm sick and tired of you nagging at me all the time. I'm sick and tired of all this arguing. I'm sick of you! I'm sick of me. Sick, sick, sick! Sick of all of it!" He chugged the glass of Brandy he had poured and reached for the bottle.

"You're sick all right! Sick in the head! You can't even come home one evening and treat your family like human beings!" Judith sobbed. John's eyes glazed as the whiskey took effect. His shakiness disappeared and he felt its familiar warming comfort in the pit of his stomach. He took a close look at Judith. She was a gorgeous, slender, full-breasted brunette with straight hair practically down to her waist. A dream come true. And now he had made her cry. How could he ever be so mean to her?

"Aw, Judith, sweetheart. I'm sorry. I didn't mean anything. I love you. Don't cry." He put an increasingly unsteady arm around her waist and began kissing her face. His hands began to wander.

"John...don't... Sarah - Where's Sarah!" Judith jumped up and ran out the door. "Sarah! Sarah!"

"Here, Mommy," Sarah whispered from behind the front bushes where she was holding her teddy bear's hands over its ears.

Chapter Two: Terry

The sun set suddenly leaving the desert shrouded in a gray mist with three blood-red shafts streaking across the sky like light from a hideous Jack-O-Lantern. The bright glow at the horizon had a hypnotic effect on Terry Silverman that seemed to draw him toward it. Sprawled across the lawn chair in front of his trailer, he pondered the meaning of his life. So far his main objective had been achieved: refusing to be like his Father by keeping sedated with daily doses of cough syrup and marijuana. This was his saving grace - the only way he could keep from doing what that bastard had done to his own flesh and blood. That and staying away from marriage and kids. Yeah, the desert was the best place for keeping your cool. No hassles, no relationships, only survival to deal with, and he'd had a lifetime of experience learning how to survive.

Buck trotted over from his place in the shadow of the trailer and nuzzled Terry's hand. *Must be time to eat,* Terry thought and got up to get Buck a can of dog food. Halfway to the trailer he stopped and heard the evening call of one lone coyote. *Coyote is alone, too, where he can't hurt anyone.*

Terry remembered his last few months in the city, Miswalkie, a big mid-western metroplex with a small-town mentality. It was his hometown, but it never seemed like home. He had always felt like an alien walking in a strange land in a fruitless search for something warm and familiar, something he could identify with, something that made sense, but always coming up empty. He had pretty much given up that search as a young man when he discovered relief from all mental and emotional conflict through the use of those magic substances: Pot, cocaine, speed, valium, booze and pretty much anything he could get his hands on that would keep him high all day, until he passed out at night, and get him going in the morning when he came to.

He thought of the car accident about ten years ago when he was twenty-three. He had mixed that wonderful muscle relaxer, Librium, with booze to the point where he lost most of his muscle control and could not walk straight. He remembered lumbering down the street with his old friend John whom he hadn't seen in a while. Laughing, falling down, trying to dance like a clown, falling down some more and laughing even harder, hard enough to hide the emotional pain he worked so hard to cover up. John told him he was walking like the scarecrow in Wizard of Oz after losing half his straw. They parted ways that night in front of Terry's store, The Smokey Pipe, and, in a booze induced blackout, got behind the wheel to go to who knows where. That 'where' was intensive care, three weeks in a coma, too many broken bones to count and a DUI with two years' probation for flying his car over an embankment, rolling it down a hill and crashing through the back of someone's garage where he was found encased in torn and twisted metal. It was six months before he was released from the hospital and back on his feet. At least he was well-supplied with prescription drugs during those times.

Ah, the Smokey Pipe. He and his old chum, Bailey Grimes. Terry really thought they had something there. Good ol' Bailey. Terry felt like they were close friends in high school, but boy he had no idea what Bailey was really like until they went into bus ness together. And he sure turned out to be a major basket case! First off, Bailey actually thought he could build a successful business by being honest and hard working. Hah! He seemed oblivious to the deceit and treachery it took to make it in the business world these days. So, Terry thought he might as well get his share, and what better business than the high profit world of drug dealing? Life is just a struggle for survival that ends in misery anyway so why not go for whatever you can, to hell with the risks. He talked Bailey into going along with it and things seemed to go well for a short while. But Bailey had to go and have some religious experience and turn into one of those 'born agains'. Then he wanted to change the head shop into a legitimate business. He was even going to start a church in the back room! Ten years rolling in high profits dealing drugs down the toilet because Bailey had to go and get religion! He agreed to his partner's buy out and tried to deal drugs in the city, but that didn't last long. Religious boy decided to clear his conscience to the police, so Terry had no choice but to leave town in a hurry. When he stopped running, he was in Arizona, Navajo territory, with a burned-up engine and six-thousand dollars cash. He'd always wanted to live the simple life anyway and what better place than in the desert.

The first star appeared in the desert sky. It was big and bright and a little bit reddish. *Must be Mars,* he thought. Terry remembered when he was a kid and he and his best friend John would be playing outside after dinner. Terry always took seeing that first star very seriously. *I wish I may, I wish I might, have the wish I wish tonight.* His wish was always the same though he never told anyone about it, not even his best friend: *no one should ever find out what happens in our house.* That's why he spent so many weekends sleeping over at John's. Only once did John stay at his house and that was when dear old Dad was off hunting. Thank God for the hunting trips so he and his five brothers and sisters could have a little peace once in a while.

Especially his sisters. No little girl should ever have to be victimized like that. He felt guilty that he was unable to stop his Dad and was afraid he could end up just like him. He pushed it out of his mind as he always did by guzzling the rest of his bottle of cough syrup.

Mom was a jewel. He loved his Mom and wished he could be with her right now. She spent all her time taking care of the kids and did her best to keep Dad at bay. But Dad was so unpredictable he could never be tamed. He was going to do what he was going to do whenever he felt like it. Damn anyone else's feelings. He was like Hitler with seven hostages. *Hitler and the seven hostages. Sounds like a fairy tale.* Terry chuckled to hide the pain.

He opened the can of dog food at both ends and watched the perfectly cylindrical shape fall into the dog dish. As usual, Buck picked it up whole and dropped it on the ground nuzzling it around until it was thoroughly covered with sand and dirt. *I guess he doesn't like that factory can taste either.* Terry went into the trailer to get another bottle of cough syrup and his bong.

Chapter Three: John

John was running down a dry creek bed just two steps ahead of the creature. It was huge but indistinct. All he had to do was get to his F-101 and shoot the creature with the machine guns mounted in the wings. His legs began to feel heavy. He could barely move them. The creature was almost on top of him, his jet only ten more feet away. But his legs would no longer move. *Air raid siren. Good. Reinforcements should be here any minute.* But the creature – he felt its hot moist breath on the back of his neck and turned to see its mouth wide open, thousands of huge jagged teeth and he screamed –

John jerked upright covered in perspiration. The alarm was ringing. Judith was nowhere in sight. He saw his ghostly image in the mirror across the room with two glassy orbs set deep inside two sunken black holes starring back at him. A wave of nausea and dizziness overtook him.

"Jude." God his head hurt. "Jude!" No answer. He stumbled into the bathroom and almost fell into the toilet. He stood there teetering trying to focus enough to aim his penis. "Jude!!" Still no answer. He fell to his knees and filled the toilet bowl with a bucketful of last nights 'fun'.

His stomach and brain sloshed as he stumbled into the upstairs hall and called out once more. The house seemed startlingly quiet. It felt empty. A gurgle in his gut released the last vestige of substance on his insides. Time seemed to stand still as he floated bodiless down the stairs.

In the kitchen, the refrigerator loomed before him cold and lifeless waiting to give up its goods to the next sufferer. On the door was a crudely crayoned house with awkward skewed windows and a misshapen front door. A lone curl of smoke came out of the chimney and began making a circle around the house. It circled again and again until the house looked like a spiraling circle of gray smoke spinning into a vortex. The refrigerator began to spin with the picture until the entire room was spinning into a hazy blur. He closed his eyes tight and pressed the heels of his hands hard against his temples. When he opened them again the refrigerator was still and the house had only one lone curl of smoke coming out of its chimney. He contemplated the illegible signature Sarah had scribbled across the bottom. He would have smiled had he not been so consumed with his own misery. He opened the door and pulled out the juice pitcher. *V8 with a shot of vodka. That should do it. Just one shot should be enough.*

John opened the cabinet above the refrigerator and reached for the Smirnoff he had disguised in the olive oil bottle. Vodka was his daytime go to booze because it didn't smell like whiskey and he felt he could cover up his breath with mints and fool everyone. There was a note scotch-taped to the neck of the bottle. *Oh my god! She found my stash!* His heart pounding in his chest, he stood staring past the note into the silence and decided to have his drink before reading it. He sat at the table and poured the thick red liquid into last night's glass. It was like leftovers from a bloody battle. He topped off the glass with the vodka and quickly guzzled his medicine. Feeling a little less shaky he was ready to focus on the note.

What you did last night is unforgivable. We are gone forever.

"Oh god, oh god, oh god, oh god!" His heart was pounding again. His whole body felt paralyzed and hollow. "Oh, shit! What have I done! Oh god!"

John slumped back in the kitchen chair and thought hard. He remembered coming home, arguing about Sarah. A couple of drinks. Dinner. No, he didn't remember dinner. Something about Sarah disappearing. *Holy crap, did she get hurt?* No, that wasn't it. Jude found her in the bushes. But what happened after that? He could not remember a thing. His memory was blank.

Nothing else was written on the paper. *Unforgivable? Gone forever?* If only he knew what had happened. He felt the panic of a boy who was in really big trouble and was about to get the whooping of his life. He thought about calling her Mom and his stomach felt like it would jump out of his throat. It was seven forty-five, time to get dressed and go to work. His job at the Family Advocacy Center could wait. He had to figure this thing out. What did he do? Where did they go? How could he fix this? He didn't even know how it was broken. He sat down and poured another drink.

Maybe she found out about Brandy? But how? He only slept with Brandy a few times and she lived out of town. Brandy was cute and the moments with her felt safe and comfortable, but he knew it was wrong. She was lonely, a single Mom with a seven-year old boy who needed a male role model. He could be that man. He was really helping *her* out after all, relieving her loneliness, joking around with her son and making him laugh, if only for a few moments at a time. Maybe he said something to Jude in his blackout. *Oh god! She knows about the booze, maybe she knows about the women?* Brandy was just the latest, and he really thought he fell for her. He tried to count the women before her in his head. Four? Five? And what about during the blackouts? He looked at the phone. They'd be expecting

49

him at the staff meeting at eight-thirty. He'd never make it on time now. He felt the warmth of the vodka in the pit of his stomach. It felt safe and comfortable, if only for a few moments.

"Well, I guess it's just you and me, eh kid?" John said rhetorically to the vodka and began drinking out of the bottle. He never made it to the phone.

Chapter Four: Terry

Terry awoke suddenly to a cold gray dawn. His senses seemed hyper-alert as he lay motionless listening for what had woken him. The wind-up clock sounded like the hammering of a steel mill. Buck's heavy breathing reminded him of the time he and John got stoned in the dorm at John's college and mimicked the sound of his sleeping roommate's breathing by echoing each breath. He almost laughed out loud but remembered he was searching for what had startled him from his sleep. He started to rise but the sound of his sleeping bag rustling was so loud he froze in a half-sitting position for what seemed like an eternity. He listened intensely - the scampering of a desert mouse across the sand, the hollow cooing of a morning dove, the faint cry of a rooster from Broken Wing's small sheep ranch across the distant arroyo.

He thought of Broken Wing who grew up on the Rez and got his name from the time he fell off the wall in front of Tribal Headquarters in Shiprock while his parents were inside at some tribal meeting about mining. Broken Wing was about twelve years old and feeling like an all-powerful 'know-it-all' as he put it, showing off in front of the other waiting kids and pretending to be the clever and mischievous Coyote prancing back and forth on top of the wall. All the kids were laughing at his imitation of the Prankster when he lost his footing. They laughed even harder as he fell howling all the way. He said he didn't cry. He never cried. He stood up and tried to laugh as he walked into the building for help. His arm was in a cast for six weeks and his sister, Little Feather, painted a beautiful design of a bird's wing on it, so beautiful, he says, that he can still picture every little line and color.

Broken Wing told Terry he had been reckless in his youth but never went into any more detail other than mentioning a few times in jail for drunk and disorderly, a home life he refused to speak of, and the rejection of his parents and family. When he talked about being like Coyote, his eyes shined. He dreamed of himself as clever and resourceful, able to provide creative new ideas to help his people out of their poverty. The uranium mining for the past few decades had built hopes for his people to make some money, but that had never come to pass. The mining companies took almost all the profits and the government did little to protect his people and stand up for their rights. They were left with disease and death from all kinds of radiation poisoning.

Broken Wing had not been able to come up with any way to help and had given up trying years before he met Terry. Instead of being Coyote, he had become Lone Wolf, retreating from the fight he felt powerless against. Terry didn't understand why intellectually, but he felt it, and he felt for Broken Wing. He figured something had happened to alienate him from his people that was more like being misunderstood and unappreciated than being a bad person, and Broken Wing understood the same of Terry. They partied together around Terry's campfire two or three times a week and Broken Wing once said Terry was the only true friend he had. Although they never shared the sordid details of their past, they felt a kinship that comes from being on the same horrific boat, shipwrecked and left alone on a desert island. Theirs was an understanding of unspoken evil deeds accepted and forgiven in each other's presence.

"Buck," Terry whispered from his frozen pose. Buck opened his eyes and lifted his head toward Terry with a look like, *what is it now, paleface, I'm dreaming about Fifi.* Terry reasoned that if there was somebody out there, Buck would have already been barking at the trailer door. Terry sat up all the way.

"Hello," he said tentatively. No response. "Hello," he said again into the silence.

"I must be going wacko, Buck. Eh, Buck ol' buddy." Buck began wagging his tail and stood up and greeted Terry with a huge sloppy lick on the chin. "Sure, you'd protect me, wouldn't you? There's nobody here." Still, he couldn't help but wonder what could have possibly woken him. He

searched his mind for answers. What had he been dreaming? He couldn't remember. He did remember skipping dinner and replacing it with his smoke and 'tea'. He shuttered at the thought of downing a whole bottle of cough syrup and looked around for something to eat that would calm his stomach into drinking another bottle.

He knew the cupboard was empty. He hadn't gone to town for over a week. He opened the ice chest to find one lone pickle spear floating among chunks of unknown debris and a torn ice bag. His mind wandered to the time when he and John had a brief reunion about eight years out of high school. They had gone to the Edgewater Resort on O'Connell Lake drunk out of their minds to rent a motorboat in order to go joy riding. Old man Turtenwald would have none of that, but they finally convinced him to rent them one of his old heavy wooden rowboats. They rowed and drank until they passed out.

What a day! When the boat hit the shore, the jolt woke them up. They were so sunburned he vaselined blisters for days afterward. Terry thought hard about that and realized that may have been the last time he saw John, maybe eight or ten years ago. He did remember reading an article in the back of the Sentinel about John Whitlock, son of Carl Whitlock of Whitlock's Grab 'n' Go stores, disappearing, but

he never heard what happened to him. Terry felt a pang of guilt about not trying to find him after that. He knew John could never find *him* because even when he lived in the city, he moved around too much and never rented a place or got a phone in his own name. In fact, their communication had been sporadic since childhood, yet John always seemed to show up when something happened to him. Like coming to the hospital after that near fatal crash where he broke half the bones in his body. There was John, his cherubic face smiling at him as he awoke from a coma. In fact, they celebrated his recovery on that rowboat a few weeks after his release from the hospital.

Well he wasn't in a coma now and everything was quiet. The rooster crowed a second time. Terry stretched and got up to look around for his bong. *Hmmm, must have left it outside.* Suddenly, as if a hundred events converged into a single moment, the screen door sprung open, an arm holding a pistol appeared in the doorway, the trailer filled with shouts and khaki uniforms, and Terry was thrust to the floor on his face with a foot on his head and his arms pinned behind him.

"Terry Silverman, you're under arrest."

Terry was terrified. He was no stranger to hearing his rights read and feeling the cuffs behind his back. But he was beginning to come to his senses. He was beginning to feel. My God, he was beginning to feel! He needed his morning dose! He began writhing as if in great agony, struggling against the four strong hands that gripped him tightly while trying to slap on handcuffs. Buck jumped into action tearing at the invaders arms and biting deeply.

"Bu-u-u-uck! Bu-u-u-ck!" Terry's high-pitched screams pierced the morning sky painting it blood red. Two federal officers were no longer enough to hold down the compulsion of this enraged lean and wiry addict.

A loud shotgun blast came from somewhere outside the trailer, the two officers to hit the floor, and pointed their guns at the open door. Another blast blew the door off its hinges and sent glass and debris flying everywhere. They shot blindly into the opening. Within moments another blast came through the other side of the trailer making a new hole above the stove. The officers lay back-to-back shooting in both directions. Terry took a flying leap, bounced off his bed, crashed through the trailer's rear window and rolled across the desert floor. Buck was right behind him like a bullet through the broken window. Another shotgun blast, this time from the front of the trailer. Broken Wing's smiling face appeared quickly from the side. Terry began to cry out, but Broken Wing motioned him to silence as he ran out into the desert waving with his shotgun for Terry to follow. Within seconds they jumped down a six-foot embankment into an arroyo where Broken Wing's old pick-up sat idling and ready. Terry started to cry out for Buck, but Broken Wing slapped his hand over Terry's mouth. "Buck can take care of himself." They could still hear the pistol shots from the direction of the trailer as they sped off toward the mountains.

"You got yourself into a peck a trouble this time, eh Kokopelli?" Broken Wing only called Terry 'Kokopelli' when he was amused, and Terry's insanity seemed to amuse him quite often. He first met Terry seven months ago, a tall wiry figure dancing contortions around a campfire in front of his trailer like an Indian in an old 'B' western. It was more curiosity than common courtesy to visit the new arrival as there were so few living in the high desert and no one had moved up there in years. "You practicin' for an audition, Kokopelli?" were Broken Wing's first words probably because Terry's gangly contortions looked like the image of the flute-playing muse with his wild spastic movements.

Terry slowed down and laughed, imitated blowing on a flute, tripped and rolled on the ground in drunken ecstasy. They spent their first evening together sharing a bong and telling non-sensical stories of ancient times and desert fantasies in surrealistic streams of consciousness flowing like a peyote ceremony.

"I guess there's a few things I never told you," Terry panted under his breath.

"I'm not stupid, Kokopelli. I know you got to live same as me. We're cut from the same cloth, you and me. A Dad we hate. People that don't understand us. A world out to get us. No one to turn to."

"Well I got you, Broken Wing. You are a true blue friend and now you're in as much trouble as I am."

"Troubles aren't always what they seem. My life is always trouble. Trouble with no way out. No solutions. I always thought maybe we could find a solution together, you know, as blood brothers. There's got to be some way out. Maybe we can find it up in the mountains."

"It's gonna be much worse if we get caught." Terry was shaking now from adrenaline and drug withdrawal. He reached into his pocket for his secret 'go to' cure but found no cough syrup.

"You think we could stop at a drugstore?" Terry asked seriously.

"Oh, Kokapelli!" was the response and Broken Wing turned onto Navajo Road 36 and headed east toward the Chuska Mountains.

Chapter Five: John

John Whitlock's eyes opened to white lights flickering in a sea of darkness. The floor was shaking to a loud rumble and his body was being jostled violently from side to side. His head seemed detached from his body as he looked around unable to move. There was a loud metallic screech and he slid forward as if sledding down a grassy hill on a piece of cardboard. His feet hit something hard as he jerked to a stop with an echoed 'thunk'. He lifted his head a few inches and the lights began dancing more vigorously now in swirls. His brain bounced against the inside of his skull and he groaned.

He sat up carefully groping in the darkness and gingerly nursing his aching head. The floor continued to shake so he more or less crawled in the direction of one of the dancing lights. Through the deafening noise came the three-toned harmony of a train whistle sounding in a minor key. Trying to pull his wits together, he peered into the little crack of light.

The world through the crack was moving by at a dizzying rate. Trees, rocks, telephone poles, bushes were whirling by as if being sucked into a black hole somewhere behind him. He thought he saw a mountain range off in the distance. He closed his eyes and continued to see swirls of black madness rushing around him in a crescendo of chaos until he doubled over and vomited. Rolling onto his back John moaned himself back to unconsciousness as the floor rumbled on.

"Hey! Yo! In there! Get up!" John's eyes shot open only to be attacked with a two-ton force of white light. Through the pounding brightness he could make out the silhouette of something that looked like an E.T. "I'm talkin' to you asshole! Get the hell outta there!"

John raised his head slightly to see another figure coming through the light like a demon from another dimension. The E.T. and the demon landed next to him, grabbed his arms and jerked him to his feet. He was unable to resist. His whole body felt weak and helpless. The two creatures threw him into the brightness, and he crashed into something that felt like bushes and rolled to a stop against a stand of prickly pear cactus. He looked up to see two men standing inside the door of an open boxcar and waving sardonically, as the freight train they were attached to started moving away.

John sat up in the middle of what looked like a desert. His heart was beating rapidly as he moved from confusion to panic. There was not a tree in sight; only scattered yucca and ocotillo surrounded by scrub brush, gravel and sand with green islands of prickly pear dotting the landscape. In the distance against a hazy bluish-gray sky were the outlines of mountains edging the desolate wasteland of which he was now a citizen. His mouth was dry; he rubbed his unshaven face and scratched his head. His hair felt matted and dirty. The white t-shirt he was wearing was filthy and torn in several places. He recognized the gray Harley sweatpants his sister had given him and reached into its only pocket and came up empty. He was wearing shoes, thank god, Reebok runners with all the laces intact. A breeze blew dust and sand all around him burning his eyes. He doubled over coughing and sputtering until bile dripped down his chin. He dry-heaved, his stomach was completely empty.

He propped himself up feebly on one arm and watched as the train disappeared down the tracks until the desert became silent. The desolation felt oddly familiar, a manifestation of a repressed feeling he had been carrying with him for a long time. His heartbeat banged in his ears as he realized for the first time in his life that he was truly lost and alone.

The dull silver-gray sky hid the sun and there were no buildings or roads in sight. The distant mountains looked inviting, like a place where he might crawl off to die. Maybe there was a lush green valley paradise hidden behind those peaks with a clear flowing creek snaking off into the distance and a soft mossy bank on which he could lay his tortured body. A turkey vulture left its circling pattern and headed toward the mountains. John pushed himself onto his knees. Spots filled his vision until he almost blacked out again. He shook his head and felt his brain bang against his skull and yelped in pain. Somehow, he managed to get up to a standing position and stumble forward. He moved slowly toward the mountains, step by step, sick with pain.

The mind is a complex finely tuned mechanism and, when faced with life or death, can do an amazing job of protecting the body and the human psyche. Unable to think rationally, his intellect still mostly numbed from alcohol, John was propelled only by his survival instincts. He seemed to separate from his body and float forward humble and weightless. As he moved, he fixated on the mountain range. As if he were watching a movie, he saw giant projections of his precious daughter Sarah and his wife Judith against one of the mountainsides. Judith was waving that horrible goodbye note she had left at what seemed to be a different time and another dimension. *What you did! We are gone forever!* He saw Sarah floating on a column of smoke pouring out of a large chimney. 'Daddy, I love you,' *she* seemed to say, and then she was a tiny baby, floating upward in the smoke and disappearing into a dark gray cloud. *Daddy!* Judith's voice came pleading out of the cloud: 'You left us! You deserted us!' And then it was the voice of his first wife, Jane. 'I loved you, you bastard! Look at what you did to me! You are lower than worm-slime, lower than worm-slime, lower than worm-slime!' Voices from his past boomed across the desert echoing back from all directions.

A giant green worm with yellow stripes appeared before him and reared up its head, opened its mouth and spit out baby after baby, each one screaming in terror. As the babies dissolved into him one by one, his heart felt heavier and heavier. He felt so heavy he fell on the ground and passed out in a morass of guilt and self-loathing.

When he came to, the hallucinations were gone and his mind was a little clearer, but he felt weak and had the shakes. He had no idea how long he had been out. He reasoned he had been having alcohol-related delirium tremens, or DT's as his Social Work colleagues called them. The sky was bright, but the sun was still hidden behind silver-gray clouds. John had no sense of direction, no sense of time and no idea where civilization might be. It was not very hot which might indicate morning meaning he would probably have to endure the afternoon heat. His tongue felt wooly and he may not have had water for a long time. The alcohol had most likely caused dangerous dehydration.

He looked again at the distant mountain range and collected his thoughts. *This may be high desert,* he thought. *That would explain the cooler temperatures.* The mountains did not look far away, but as John stumbled forward, they did not seem to appear any closer. He stopped and looked behind him and had a vague memory of being thrown out of a train. He wondered what happened to the railroad tracks, but they were nowhere in sight now. He scanned the entire horizon and didn't see even one telephone pole or power line. The only bearing he could get was from the mountains. He licked his dry lips with a chalky tongue. *There could be water up there,* he hoped. He fixated on the mountains. His mind needed to cling to something that made sense. He felt his determination building. His desire to survive was strong and was carrying him through his weakness. He stopped and peered at the closest mountaintop through drips of perspiration. *Is that a tower? Yes! A tower!* He knew of watch towers in forests and, if this was one of those, the mountains must be forested, and that could mean water, a ranger and rescue.

Just as he was thinking this, he noticed a cloud of dust between him and the mountains. It looked stationary except that it was growing larger. Within a few moments, he could hear the sound of a car engine roaring loudly with no muffler. He started to wave his arms frantically but the vehicle was headed straight to him, so he propped himself against a large rock and waited.

After about five minutes, a rust bucket of a dune buggy came to a sliding halt in front of him and, out of a cloud of dust, a skinny gray thick-bearded man wearing a tattered straw cowboy hat winked at him and said, "Ya' got a mall 'round here, sonny?"

Chapter Six: Terry

Terry sat silently in the passenger seat of Broken Wing's truck as they sped down the open highway. No one was following them. That was good. Probably the Feds hadn't even seen their truck. Broken Wing was tapping his fingers on the steering wheel and chanting a tune in Navajo. He figured it was probably from a ceremony for having a safe journey or something like that. This middle-aged Navajo who had befriended him when he ran away to the Arizona desert was now putting his own life in jeopardy to save him. To Terry, it hardly seemed worth it. He had screwed up his entire life, amounted to nothing and was going nowhere. Not exactly a life worth saving. But Broken Wing was Navajo, and the Navajos had different ways. They had no word for revenge, and generally treated aberrant behavior like an illness rather than condemning the perpetrator and seeking retaliation. They called it the Dark Wind, and those who did not respond to curing ceremonies were sometimes banished from the tribe, yet not in anger but with compassion. Terry wasn't sure if it was forgiveness or something else, but Broken Wing's loyalty to him seemed to come, at least partly, from the Navajo Way.

Broken Wing seemed to know well the old ways of his people, yet he also knew how to party, and he and Terry had many rip-snorters together around Terry's campfire. Broken Wing had a large extended family but had never married. He had seen the local jail cell a number of times for drunk and disorderly but nothing more serious than that. He had sincerely expressed to Terry how he revered the Navajo Ways and wished he could learn to be a part of the Medicine Way and heal people. But he said he felt like a black sheep and acted out the part through drunkenness and alienating behavior. His people didn't banish him, but they didn't go out of their way to be around him either. Knowing the Navajo ways a little, Terry figured there were some that prayed for Broken Wing's healing from the effects of the Dark Wind.

"I know a little hogan just this side of the Chuska Mountains in Chinle Valley." Broken Wing knew every arroyo, mountain and patch of desert in the area and had easily escaped the sight of the officers before they could even scramble to their jeep.

"That's around the uranium mines, isn't it?" asked Terry.

"Yeah, there are abandoned mines all over the area. But there was this old Navajo, lived in this really old cabin up there til he died back in the 1950's. Some say he lived to 120 or more."

"His *chinde* must be long gone, hey?"

"Maybe. Maybe not. His name was Sadoval. They say he was around in the Indian wars and stole a cavalryman's horse. Seems the bilegaana cavalry came to make a treaty with the Dine and it didn't work out so well. This Navajo, Narbona was in charge. He was the richest Navajo who got the respect of all the Dine by winning a couple a big battles against the Mexicans. One in the Chuskas at Beesh Lichii'l Bigiizh, what we now call Narbona Pass. But after that, twenty-four Navajo leaders who had been traveling under a flag of truce to a peace conference were massacred by the Mexicans. The Americans came and finally drove out the Mexicans for good.

"So, in 1849, Narbona went with three hundred warriors to Red Rock Valley to meet Colonel Washington and his soldiers. They worked out a treaty but as the peace council broke up Sadoval began riding a horse back and forth between the soldiers and the Navajos shouting to break the treaty and attack. One of the soldiers said the horse was his and to give it back. Sadoval refused and took off so Colonel Washington stepped in and demanded the horse be turned over. Washington told his troops to set up their cannons and get ready to fire if the Navajos didn't return the horse.

Narbona, sticking up for his people, said the horse was not stolen and the shooting begun. Narbona was killed and Sadoval escaped into the Chuskas and lived there, shunned by the people for maybe over a hundred years."

"How could anyone live alone like that in a little shack in the desert?" Terry interjected sincerely.

"Look who's talking. Anyway, he was supposed to have worked for a little while in the Uranium mines. A prospector named Paddy Martinez, maybe you know about him, the guy who discovered the biggest deposit of uranium in New Mexico. Anyway, Paddy is said to have seen an old Indian working in the mines who disappeared one day. No one knew where he lived or where he went. Some say he had a vision that bad things were coming to the Dine so he left the mines to sing and dance the healing ceremonies to save the people. They say he learned the medicine ways guided by the spirits of the old ones. Soon after he left the ghosts appeared, the ghosts of the Navajos as they died from radiation. Working conditions in the mines were bad. The first ghosts began to appear from the 'red lungs. Leetso, the yellow monster, had released evil into Dine'tah."

"Yeah. Over at the library, I read that back in the fifties, miners, millers, truckers, and their families, mostly Navajo, were exposed to high radiation levels even for 1950's standards. The 'ghosts' were the victims of all kinds of cancer and lung diseases caused by over exposure to radiation and radon gases. Even the livestock was tainted and many of your people's homes were built from brick and mortar made from radiation drenched sands that washed down from the mines. I read there are still maybe a thousand abandoned mines and exposed uranium 'tailings' all over the reservation from Utah, through Arizona and here in the Chuskas and into New Mexico," Terry exhorted having spent a little time in the Navajo library during one of his grocery trips to Window Rock. He had begun to develop a feeling of kinship to the Navajo because of his friendship with Broken Wing and wanted to learn more about these people. They were innocent victims of the man, too, and probably carried unresolved resentment and pain from their victimization just like Terry carried his childhood pain into adulthood. Both hated and feared authority. He looked upon all authority as self-centered persecutors preying on the weaker and more helpless, just as his Dad had preyed upon his sisters. Until he had moved near their reservation, he had not known the extent of Navajo exploitation in modern times by large energy interests in collaboration with certain government agencies like the Bureau of Atomic Energy. But, just as in his childhood, he felt powerless to do anything about it, and stayed high instead. He and Broken Wing were a perfect match in their misery.

"They say Sadoval danced the Medicine Way alone every day up to the end. He never stopped loving his people even though they shunned him. Funny thing though. No one ever found his body, or a grave or anything. I supposed if you really live that long, maybe you got special powers or something that can spirit you away."

Broken Wing's story had distracted Terry temporarily but the desire to get high reared its ugly head. He would like to stop taking drugs but saw no other way. In fact, the only time he had ever stopped was when he was in the hospital, but they gave him lots of pain killers, he made sure of that, which means he was never really clean from drugs. Terry pined the loss of his trailer and his dog, but he knew he could never go back there just like he could never go back to his hometown. He never meant any harm. He just wanted to stay high all the time and it was easier to deal drugs to support his own habit. He figured he must have been involved with some pretty big wheels for the Feds to track him all the way to Arizona. All he knew was he bought and sold and never much paid attention to the identity of the sellers, and the buyers of what he didn't keep for himself were usually people he knew or friends of friends. Sources were best kept secret. The less he knew, the less the risk of being implicated. He probably had not been straight since junior high school. This gnawed at him in sober moments, but he always had something to take to numb the guilt feeling of wasting his life away. If there were no drugs there was booze. If he couldn't get booze, he could always find a grocery or drug store that sold cough syrup. He was beginning to panic. How was he going to get high now?

They reached pavement and turned right onto Navajo Highway 12 heading north. "Hey, Broken Wing, ya got any weed?"

Chapter Seven: John

"A what?" John was still dazed and wasn't sure he heard the high-pitched tinny voice correctly.

"Ya' got a mall around here?! A mall, man, a mall! I got a hankerin' fer one a them big soft pretzels."

"Pretzels?"

"You know they taste best with plain yellow mustard on 'em. That's how I like 'em. Plain yellow mustard. Yep. Ya want one? Hop in. Must be a mall 'round here someplace."

John robotically obeyed and walked around to the other side of the buggy and stared inside. The passenger seat and floor were covered in wrappers from all kinds of candy bars, donuts and almost any sweet treat you could imagine along with dozens of smashed empty orange soda cans.

"Well come on, come on! Git in! I ain't got all day! Shove that shit on the floor an' set! Careful! Don't wanna litter the desert now!" He waved his arm carelessly then reached into a cooler in the back seat and pulled out a can of orange soda.

John dragged himself up on the seat while pushing trash to the floor. The movement made him dizzy and he almost passed out again. The odd man tapped his fingers on the wheel and hummed an almost unrecognizable version of Sympathy for the Devil. Out of this humming came, in a very sly voice, "Pleased to meet you. Won't you guess my name. What's puzzlin' you is the nature of my game." The old man paused and handed John the soda. The can felt cold and moist and John frantically opened it and guzzled.

"Hey, slow down a bit, padnuh," the old man said with concern in his voice. He suddenly changed his demeanor and sent a starry gaze toward the sky and sighed, "Here I am draggin' you out of another scrape." Then with a chuckle, "Nothin' to worry 'bout tho'. You got a long ways to go afore you finish this life."

"Huh?" is all John could manage. This did not make any sense at all. He wondered if he was having DT's again. No. The wondering convinced him he wasn't.

"Well look here Johnny, this ain't no swamp but yer stuck in a pile a' muck anyway. Ya' ain't got no idea where ya' been, where ya' are or where ya' headed do ya?" A thoughtful pause was followed by a cheerful, "Hey ya' want to know where ya' been?"

"S-s-sure," John stuttered, and his dizzy racing mind began to focus. He thought of his first wife, Jane and how he had deserted her in a drunken blackout. Sure, he had contacted her six months later and told her where he was. He tried to make amends, but he was too scared and self-absorbed to do much so they agreed on a divorce and he started a new life sober in Austin, Texas, over a thousand miles away. That new life had hope and promise. It led to a college degree, a new career, another marriage and a beautiful daughter. Unfortunately, try as he might, he could not resist taking that first drink again even after seven years of sobriety. The drinking quickly turned into an obsession. After only six months of it, here he was coming out of a drunken blackout in the middle of nowhere having probably drank away his job, his family and his sanity.

"Looks plenty sad don't it Johnny," said the old man.

"Hey, how do you know my name and what's going on here!"

"O, nothin' much, Johnny, just lookin' fer a pretzel. Ya know I like the way they're all twisted into such a funny shape from just one long piece. You kin start on one end and follow all the twists 'n turns until ya git t'other. Course it's always hard to resist wrappin' yer teeth around the middle. It's a big soft squishy knot and sometimes ya just have close yer eyes and take a big bite. Careful, tho' or you'll git a squish a mustard in yer eye." He started laughing and his laughter built up like the crescendo of a Stravinsky symphony until his eyes were tearing.

"Look! I appreciate the ride. You probably saved my life! But what in God's name is going on here?!"

"Funny thing, Johnny. I often wonder if God's got a name..."

"Hey! Watch out!" John shouted. They went flying over a six-foot-deep embankment into an arroyo and came to an abrupt halt in a cloud of dust.

"Whoooweee! Love this desert! It looks all the same at first peek 'til ya' get to movin'! Never know what to expect when yer movin'." He turned the buggy toward the far side of the arroyo and headed straight to it at full speed.

"Aaah! What are you nuts!? Stop! Stop it! Stop!"

The man slammed on the brakes, skidded sideways and skillfully maneuvered to a halt right alongside the arroyo wall. As the cloud of dust swirled away in the wind, he looked John straight in the eyes and said, "Gotcha sober didn't it?"

John realized he was no longer dizzy, his head had cleared, and he actually felt completely normal. He licked his lips and felt a moist tongue slide smoothly along them. He wasn't thirsty and actually felt quite content to be alive *and* in one piece.

"So where's this mall. I could use a clean shirt." John chided.

"Hey, Johnny, you do have a sense a humor." The man shifted his dialect from old crazy hybrid cowboy hippie to an articulate mid-western lawyer voice. "The time has come to come to grips. Do you know where you have been?"

"You *were* putting me on. I knew it! You're not crazy at all!"

"Look behind ya' Johnny."

John turned around to see a half-crazed javelina charging their vehicle. He instinctively jumped out and tried to scramble up the loose rock and sand of the embankment glancing back at the fast approaching animal. As he struggled unsuccessfully, the man sat calmly behind the wheel, took out a stick, held it like a rifle and went 'pow, pow

pow' at the enraged animal. It stopped dead in its tracks, turned around and walked back from where it came.

John slumped down in a dusty heap on the arroyo floor. "What the hell…"

"Hell got nothin' ta do with it. She's jus' tryin' ta protect her brood. I wuz jus' explainin' ta her we ain't gonna go nowhere near her kids. We's jus' lookin' fer a pretzel."

"Now look here Doctor Doolittle," John panted, "I don't know what stopped that animal from attacking but using a stick like a gun sure didn't do it."

"Ya sure 'bout that, Johnny? You and Terry used a lot of sticks fer guns when you was kids playin' army in the dirt."

John hadn't thought about that in years and it sent his mind into a myriad of childhood scenes with Terry and him finding a new house construction site with piles of dirt or an open field with a creek. They almost never used man made toys. They were perfectly content to find the ideal piece of wood or stick that held like a WWII machine gun. And they always started out with a platoon of men until the enemy whittled it down to just the two of them. John loved that feeling of being the last two brave warriors successfully beating down an entire company of Nazi's. It was simpler with just the two of them, fewer variables, no one to worry about, because they were invulnerable and super courageous.

"Hey, how did you know about Terry?"

"Oh, I know a lot of things about a lot of people, but they only come up when they are needed," and the old man changed to his lawyer voice. "And right now, you needed that memory - a time when you had a friendship that went deep, when you cared for and were cared about without asking any questions. Unqualified friendship, or, as the psychologists call it, unconditional love."

For reasons as yet unknown to John, the conversation with this strange man no longer seemed odd. John felt quite relaxed and comfortable. He forgot momentarily that he was in the open desert, far away from the home he destroyed and the reality that felt like a nightmare. The old man put the dune buggy in gear and the two of them moved across the desert in contemplative silence. It was comfortably familiar being a dynamic duo again, and John's mind was blissfully blank as he gazed across the desert toward the approaching mountains.

"Hey, Johnny, afore we git to the mall, I got someone I want ya ta meet, waddaya say?"

"Look, there's not going to be any mall out here and if you think there's people to meet you *are* crazy! There's nothing but this rocky desert for miles."

Just as he finished speaking, the dune buggy pulled to a stop at the base of a five-hundred-foot cliff, a cliff that had not been there a moment before. John peered up and saw a man near the top stranded on a ledge. He was shouting down at them and waving his hand.

Chapter 8: Terry

"A few more miles should do it!" Broken Wing shouted through the roaring engine and rattling of the pick-up truck as they struggled up a steep rocky slope. They had turned off the paved highway hours ago and, after a few short jogs down Navajo Service roads, started on a rugged path up the mountains that followed a long stretch of high-tension wires. "It's the straightest way up the Chuskas," Broken Wing had said before they began their climb, "with maybe a few bumps along the way."

A *few* bumps! It was the worst he had ever been on. The ground was rock and shale with towers lined up like giant metal totem poles carrying high-tension wires uphill through a kind of alleyway where the trees had been cleared to make room for them. At first the trees were stunted and sparse; but now they were getting into tall pines and green grass and shrubs amidst the purple sagebrush. It actually made a clear trail, unfortunately a trail used only by utility trucks and jeeps once in a blue moon which made it a very rugged path.

It was no use shouting back. Broken Wing knew what he was doing and nothing Terry could say would help anyway. He was gripping the handle above the door perhaps a little harder than he had to as he was experiencing drug withdrawal while his body and brain were being shaken to a pulp. He didn't want to tell Broken Wing what he was going through. He was actually too ashamed to be so dependent even though he had been on this roller coaster all of his adult life. It wasn't really shame in Broken Wings eyes he was worried about, it was shame in his own eyes: shame for wasting his life away and shame for having no other recourse than to be high as much as possible for as long as he should live. And that damnable Father of his! It was his fault after all for being such a bastard. Terry did not realize that it wasn't his Father or the drugs but his own anger and resentment that kept him in bondage.

A large hole jolted them to a stop and the engine stalled.

"What the hey?!" Broken wing jumped out of the truck to survey the damage. "Axle's broke."

Terry took a deep breath and looked up toward the top of the slope. It looked lush and green up there. The towers seemed to lead the way to a heavenly kingdom, but their austere metallic frames looked foreboding to Terry, and he felt powerful, cold impersonal energy telling him that such a beautiful place was unavailable to the likes of him. He poured his viscous frame out of the truck, fell in a puddle on the ground and vomited.

"Oooh, Kokapelli, you ain't doin' so good. We gotta get you outta this hot sun." Broken Wing gave him a drink from his water bottle then dragged him around to the shady side of the truck. He pulled a backpack out of the pickup and jammed it full of plastic water bottles from an open case behind the front seat. "Can you stand up?"

"Yeah, I think so." Terry stood on rubber legs and leaned on Broken Wing. Together, they trudged up the slope in the sweltering heat following the towers to eternity. Terry's drug withdrawal was in full swing. He was nauseous, dizzy and weak. His muscles and joints were screaming in pain. He was completely dependent on Broken Wing.

At first, Terry felt Broken Wing's strong body holding him up and dragging him. He stumbled, banged his feet against rocks, stumbled again, while Broken Wing kept him from falling. He felt a great heaviness over his entire being. His mind screamed, *Mommy, Mommy! Get me out of here!* He felt like he was being compressed between layers of thick mattresses standing on end, as soft as pillows yet as hard and jagged as volcanic rock. The mattresses were swaying in motion like waves on the ocean. He felt sick, his stomach at his throat. The mattresses pressed him in tighter and tighter, the softness crushing him while the knife sharp stone cut into his skin. He moaned and sighed, going back and forth between pain and pleasure. But as they made their way up the slope, Terry felt lighter and lighter. He felt himself rising out of the nauseating torture of the mattresses, leaving them and his body behind. He seemed to be floating high above the pine covered mountains that jutted up from their high desert surroundings. Looking down, he saw two figures arm-in-arm moving in choreographed steps to the rhythm of the wind. Their identity and how he was floating high above them did not matter. His own identity had become insignificant in the face of this new experience. The wind was beating a rhythmic pattern loudly against his ears, pounding out a song that seemed to separate him from the world he had always known. His reality was transforming from the egregious struggle for survival it had always been, to something sweeter and more beautiful than he had ever imagined.

A tiny voice began humming a melody he had never heard, so softly that it might have been his imagination. The melody was like a tiny speck of sound embedded in the booming wind beat, yet it was clear, concise, consistent and, as tiny as it was, it was solid and secure. It attracted his full attention until it supplanted the loud wind song, yet it grew no louder. He heard himself humming along as if it were a familiar tune from his childhood. It gave him a sense of simpler days where the world belonged to him and he belonged to the world and he played in blissful harmony with no cares or fears.

The wind became light and cool against his face as he floated freely with arms outstretched in circles above the mountains. He felt like he could glide up there forever in comfort and peace. Slowly, he descended in diminishing circles toward the two male figures. He glided easily to the ground and stood facing Terry and Broken Wing. Physical, mental and psychic boundaries had melted away and the three were as one, whole and complete in fullness of life.

Broken wing stopped and stared at the large black bird standing in his path. Its dark piercing eyes were emitting silvery sparks that had a hypnotic effect. It was singing a soft melody, a song that was simultaneously familiar and unfamiliar. The song was vibrating in perfect harmony with his spirit, and it filled him with a great sense of joy. The bird turned its head sideways and Broken Wing stared into its eye. It was like a portal that formed into a long dark tunnel with a tiny point of light at the end. He felt like he was speeding down the tunnel to the light. The light grew larger until it opened into a lush green valley with a lazy flowing creek winding down its center, and beautiful fully leaved oak trees scattered throughout. He stepped into the valley and walked barefoot in the tall soft grass. There were brightly colored flowers scattered about of every shape and size. He sat down at the bank of the stream and listened to the sound of the light flowing water, the whisper of the breeze in the tall grass and the song... the indefinable song that seemed to sing about everything beautiful and good all at once. This was peace he had never known. Peace beyond his wildest imagination. Upstream he could see people walking toward him in single file. In the lead was a Navajo woman dressed in buckskins. She walked up to him in silence, he waved his hand in front of her and her buckskin dress turned pure white. She smiled and sat in the grass behind him. One by one the line of people came up to him, men and women. At first, they were Navajo men and women, some with noticeable injuries, others looking pained or sad. Soon he saw people of many races coming forth: clean cut men in business suits faces lined with stress, homeless people carrying layers of dirt, women in flowing dresses that looked pretty on the outside but whose eyes were hollow and strained, and children, the light almost gone from their eyes. With every person, he silently waved his hand, their clothing turned white and their injuries, pain and suffering disappeared. Everyone sat down in the grass behind him and sang the unknown melody in perfect harmony. When the line of people came to an end, Broken Wing stood up, faced the people, smiled and, in a split second the valley was gone, and he was standing once again with Terry.

"Hey, Terry...Terry...Terry!" Terry jerked up his head, opened his eyes and screeched. The bird disappeared as if it had never existed.

"Terry! Terry! I had a vision. A blackbird took me to a beautiful place. People came and everyone was changed. I felt different, too! Oh, it's just so hard to describe it!"

"Yes. I saw you by the stream. I saw everything," Terry said in a clear, calm soothing voice. He stepped away from Broken Wing and noticed a column of some kind of energy flowing down into the top of Broken Wing's head from a shimmering silver-gray cloud bank in the sky. The column flowed down his body then out from his heart to Terry's heart. He felt this flow of energy go through his body and out the top of his head melding into the shimmering cloud in the sky. Then he noticed the energy was flowing through them going both ways at once always connected to the cloud and to each other. The energy gave Terry a most wonderful feeling, like the soothing coolness of a fresh mountain stream flowing over the body after a day of sweat and toil. As it flowed, Terry felt lighter and lighter. A thousand pounds of emotional baggage stuffed with years of remorse and resentment were being lifted from him, as if they were siphoned out of him by the column of energy and absorbed by the cloud. In one timeless moment that could have been an eon, all his anger was removed along with the underlying fears that had been motivating it. Guilt was taken, then shame and loneliness, until tears streamed down his face. Layers of grief and pain were being removed so quickly he barely had time to let them go. Everything around him was swirling inside the shimmering energy-flow. At once he became conscious of this same substance radiating forth from the center of his own being, radiating out as a pure light, a light of all colors making everything glow in vivid detail around him. Terry surrendered completely to this phenomenon and sobbed uncontrollably as Broken Wing continued to speak in a strong articulate kind voice.

"There is no blackbird nor vulture nor eagle nor hawk separate from ourselves. We all fly high and free. We are freer than the wind which can blow in any direction at any speed at any time. The possibilities are endless. There is no form we can take that is permanent. Reality is unlimited. We are unlimited. We are all made of the same substance, and this substance has no beginning and no end and satisfies all human desires. You have no struggles, no pains, no past that can harm you. These are all gone. You have desired freedom from pain. You have longed for peace and happiness. Yet, up to this point, have settled for a struggle for survival. You looked only in places your mind understood and found no permanent relief. You could not find it anywhere you looked, for it is now and always has been right here in the midst of you. You cannot find what you already have. Peace, love and harmony are your birthrights. It is now and always has been your inheritance. Now you awaken to it. Peace for you is like water to the fish. He has no awareness of the water as being separate and apart from himself. He has no knowledge of being without the water. Yet the life-giving water is always there. But you, you have been as a fish who seeks the water not realizing the water is all around you. You look here and you go there seeking the water not realizing you are swimming in it and it is already in you and outside of you, and everywhere, constantly providing life and everything to support life."

Broken Wing stopped speaking and closed his eyes. Terry looked through flowing tears at his surroundings and saw everything more clearly than ever. Trees, rocks and shrubs were shimmering in spectacular detail. He distinctly saw his entire past fold into perfect harmony in the present moment. He belonged. He fit in. He had purpose. His whole being seemed to stand up tall in dignity knowing he was a part of a world that now, suddenly made sense and seemed to be going somewhere. Broken Wing's shimmering aura was like a flowing robe that blended into the landscape. He felt a bond with him now that went far beyond friendship and brotherly love. This was a bond that unified them with all mankind in love, peace, harmony and joy.

Another voice sounding like the one that came out of Broken Wing came to Terry from nowhere and from everywhere and said, "Now is your time to be as me for I am as you. There is no longer a 'you' and 'I' as all is now one. Infinite love now radiates as you. In this experience you are perfectly healed and perfectly forgiven. From this time forward you shall radiate healing, forgiveness and love which shall dissolve all their opposites into a mist that will float away into nothingness. Go now and enjoy swimming in these new waters and never worry again. It is forever full and complete and available to you, to all, for all everywhere and always."

Terry squatted, picked up a stick and wrote in the dirt:

I am.
We are.
All is.

He quickly stood up and tapped Broken Wing on the shoulder. Broken Wing fell to his knees, kissed the ground and said, "Now I know who we are." He looked up into

Terry's eyes and recognized him for the first time. He was Kokapelli, the dancing flute playing Spirit that brings joy, love, peace and forgiveness to all who would have it.

"Yes. I know, also," said Terry in his new clear kind voice. "Your broken wing is now healed, and you have become forgiveness and healing which you will take back to your people. We now radiate such a thing as we have not known before, but which is pouring out of us so strongly...I-I-I... I can't keep still anymore!"

Terry laughed out loud. He laughed hard and long. He felt awake, vibrant and alive for the first time in years. His belly was filled with butterflies. His heart was leaping for joy. It was more than just finding rescue in the desert. He wasn't dizzy, he wasn't thirsty. His body felt strong and refreshed. All his withdrawal symptoms were gone as were his cravings for drugs and cough syrup. He truly had no fear of the future, no regrets over the past and no worries. None. None whatsoever. He was so uncontrollably and ecstatically happy that he could not help but dance, dance and play Kokapelli's song.

Broken Wing sat back against a rock and looked on with amazement as a transformed Kokapelli danced and played not in the usual random out of his mind way, but in a

fantastic rhythmically accurate and complex dance with the agility and skill of the professionally trained. He danced with ease, light on his feet, making it look natural and easy. He blew on an
invisible flute that seemed to create melodies that echoed among the surrounding rock formations.

Broken Wing kept sitting and Terry kept dancing.

When the dance ended, there was the loud clanging of a triangle. A female voice called from the distance, "Time for dinner! Time for dinner! Come and eat!"

About 100 yards to the right, a grove of tall pine trees was swaying in the breeze amidst lush green grass dotted with blooming flowers. In the center of the grove was a perfectly built log cabin, smoke coming out of its tall brick chimney and a rusty old odd-looking dune buggy covered with weeds sitting next to it. The two friends accepted this as normal and natural. Everything seemed to fit perfectly without any need for explanation.

"Come let us enjoy the moment," declared Broken Wing.

"Yes.   Let's go meet our new hostess," Terry shouted joyfully. And they walked briskly to the cabin laughing all the way.

{End of First Movement]

First Interlude:

The Prospector

William Maestro screamed for help. It was all he *could* do. It was at least 500 feet straight down and 30 feet back to the top of the cliff. One wrong move and he was a goner. He paused and looked at the cliff face. There were plenty of ledges like the ones he had been climbing on, but none within reach. Above were the remnants of the one that had crumbled away under his foot. He was on his back spread eagled with room enough to roll over on his side

. A cursory examination of his body revealed no serious injuries. "Where is Allen anyway?" he thought knowing full well Allen was somewhere near the campsite looking for the canary-yellow show of uranium the Bureau of Atomic Energy had sent them out to find. That is exactly why William was in this predicament now. He was just out of college and knew he was smarter than most. Uranium was in high demand mainly for the building of nuclear weapons, so he wrote his doctoral thesis on why, when, and where uranium could be found in hopes of getting the attention of the Bureau of Atomic Energy or one of the big mining companies. His thesis proved he could find a vein here on the eastern slope of the Chuska Mountains where curiosity and a strong intuition led him down the cliff-stepped layers of stone that formed the ledges.

William screamed again. He tried to make the highest pitched sound he could hoping it would carry up the cliff and across the plateau carried by the wind to his partner. Surprisingly, he heard a response not from above, but from below. He peered over the ledge to see a tiny vehicle with two animated doll-like figures waving their arms and shouting in tightly compressed voices that were embedded deeply in the howl of the wind. He waved back and watched them get back into the vehicle and drive along the cliff face. He followed the sound of the engine as they drove out of sight and could hear it echoing higher and higher until it silenced above him.

"We've got a rope!" he heard from above and responded with an 'OK' as the rope came sailing down the cliff and landed perfectly in his hands.

"Tie it around your waist and hold on!" which he was already doing, so in a few seconds he shouted 'OK' again and the rope slowly hoisted him up to the top where two men grabbed his arms and set him safely on the ground.

William sat catching his breath and surveyed his lean muscular body - only a few bruises and scrapes on his arms, nothing sprained or broken.

"You had quite a fall. Could've been killed", said the younger of the two gentlemen in the usual manly way of stating the obvious. The older one was leaning causally on an odd-looking vehicle with no roof or windshield that had a roll bar above the back of the front seats. It was like nothing he had ever seen.

"Name's Bill," William reached out his hand and the younger man pulled him up to standing. "My epitaph could have been written right here instead of somewhere in the future as the great young man who discovered uranium in these mountains." He paused and, hearing no response, continued explaining how he was hired by the Bureau of Atomic Energy to look for uranium out here in the high desert based on a thesis he had written that showed the eastern side of the Chuskas would be just the place to find it.

"Yep, the BAE doesn't pay much, but when I find it, I *will* be famous and that could lead to riches untold." He paused again and realized he had been so caught up in his ambitions and dreams he did not even know to whom he was speaking.

"So who are you anyway?" The younger one looked to be in his thirties and, although his clothes were dirty and torn, he looked clean cut and educated. But the other one! He was an old geezer, skinny with a thick gray beard and a tattered straw cowboy hat, but not dangerous or ominous looking.

On the contrary, he had a twinkle in his eyes that was friendly and inviting. The younger one started to open his mouth, but the geezer jumped in. "Ya got that right, Willy boy. Ya' ain't 'a gonna be as famous as yer' gonna be rich. This whole area is loaded with uranium all the way over ta Ambrosia Lake. In fact, biggest discovery o' the century gonna happen this pm east a' here near Haystack Butte." He paused and shot a hollow gaze across to the eastern horizon. "Mining and radiation sure killed a lot of people tho'." He looked back at William. "Couldn't have ya dyin' taday and missin' out on all them great discoveries."

"So you're prospectors! You already know where the uranium deposits are?"

"Naw. I jus' know ma history is all."

"History?" the younger one interrupted. "How can something that hasn't happened yet be history?"

"Awww, Johnny, yer takin' time too seriously. It's a lot more flexible than you think. Why this here fellow is the late great William Maestro, discoverer of uranium deposits 'n' coal all 'round these parts and Canada in the early 1950's."

"1950's!' John exclaimed. "Are you trying to tell me that dune buggy is a time machine?!"

"Sort of," the old man said, "but that's not important right now. What *is* important is Billy boy here lives so he can go on ta make them discoveries, 'n' get rich 'n' famous 'n' write his autobiography and tell about the abuse and neglect of the Navajo people from the uranium mining. All that sickness and death from radiation was ignored for so many years. That is, until the famous William Maestro told all." The old man paused while John and William stared at him with their mouths hanging open. "Course Billy boy here has a few decades to go afore that all happens, and he's a gonna have ta' git rid 'o' all that arrogance and greediness first."

William clenched his fists and his face turned red. "Why you sorry old son of a-

"Now now, Billy boy. We'll get to that later, heh, heh." The old man chuckled. "Plus, he's gotta put a certain Navajo prospector off the trail by sendin' him toward Haystack Butte. There ain't no uranium over that way, right, Billy Boy?"

"Hey! Wait a minute! How do you know who I'm going to meet? No, wait! This is just plain crazy, old man. I think you

should go back to Happy Haven or wherever you belong." The old man smiled and winked at him which made him feel even more angry, so he turned his back and looked at John who appeared a little more rational.

"So, Johnny is your name?" asked William in an attempt to start a conversation that would make some sense.

"No, its *John* not Johnny. John Whitlock. I was lost in the desert and this old man, *whose name I don't even know," he* throws the old man a sideways glance, "found me and brought me here. By the way, where is here?"

"We are on the Navajo Reservation in the northern Chuska Mountains just about where the Lukachukai mountains start," said William.

"So-o-o where is that? I mean what country are we in?"

"You really have no idea where you are do you?" William asked rhetorically. "There must be a story behind that," he shot an angry glance at the old man and shook his head partly in disgust and partly to clear out the confusion. "Anyway, we're in northern New Mexico about 70 miles straight south of the four corners."

"Four corners... where Arizona, New Mexico, Utah and Colorado meet? My God, how did I get this far from Austin!?"

"You askin', Johnny or jus' musin'?" the old man chimed in with a mischievous yet serious tone.

"Now just wait a minute you two! I don't know what you're all about and I *am* grateful and all, but how do you know my full name and, *I haven't discovered any uranium yet! Nobody has! Not around here!*" William felt like he was being toyed with, but mostly he was covering up his fear with anger. Some of what the old man said seemed too close to the truth and some was pure nonsense. Maybe it was just a crazy old man and a poor lost soul, yet, how did that old man know his full name? And what was all this talk about the future? "Exactly where *are* you from. anyway?" he asked John.

"Well I'm from Austin, Texas and I got thrown off a-"

The old man interrupted in his articulate lawyer voice, "You see, hardly anything in this world is as it seems to our physical senses and finite minds. The more intelligent question would be, 'when are we from' yet 'when' is arbitrary, too, as 'when's' are constantly changing so quickly that, humanly, we cannot keep up."

"You made more sense speaking gibberish and I'm not even going to try and figure that one out!" shouted William. "Now I am truly grateful and appreciate you saving me from that cliff. You came along just at the right moment. But now I must get back to camp and re-group. I've got a partner there and we've got to compare our findings. I don't suppose you know which way is back to my camp?" William got his bearings. "Oh yeah." He turned away from the cliff and started walking. "Thanks again for saving my life and confusing the hell out of me!" he shouted over his shoulder as he heard the roar of an engine, tires spinning in the rocky soil, then, suddenly, dead silence. He looked around to see... nothing, not even dust. There was no sign of them or the strange vehicle. Even the rope was gone. He knelt where they had been parked and could see no tracks. The only marks in the gravely surface were his own footprints. He looked for the scrapes and bruises on his arms and saw none. It took a few minutes before he could shake it off as probably a bit of heatstroke and resume his walk back to the campsite. Yet he always looked back on that moment as being startlingly real somewhere beyond rationality.

Three days later William Maestro heard that a Navajo prospector, Paddy Martinez, had brought a piece of uranium ore into Grants, New Mexico from Haystack Butte and discovered the largest and richest deposit ever found in the southwest.

(End of First Interlude}

Second Movement:

Into Action

Chapter One: Terry's Serenity

Mysteries are only mysteries to the seekers, the ones who are looking for something known or unknown that they do not seem to have, be it an object, a person, an idea or greater knowledge. Those who know the truth of who they are no longer concern themselves with mysteries. To them all is peace and fulfillment in the present moment. To them there is no concern over their safety and provision and no concern for what will happen next for they know that in each present moment all is provided. Their only focus is on how they can contribute to life and helping others. Their complete goal is letting the light and love pour out through them in each moment.

Terry Silverman and Broken Wing were in this state when the triangle clanged and the voice called them to dinner. Terry, not even winded from his dancing and invisible flute playing looked at Broken Wing and smiled as they entered the cabin and sat at a thick wooden table heaped with all kinds of their favorite foods. They did not look surprised, concerned or anxious. A small girl with long fluffy blond hair walked silently from the huge cast iron stove and set a bowl of steaming biscuits on the table. She kept her eyes down. She appeared calm and peaceful. There may have been a glowing shimmer of light surrounding her. At least it seemed so to Terry whose face was full of color, his cheeks rosy and his eyes sparkling like twin stars in the night.

"I see ya made it and not a minute too soon! Them biscuits ain't no good unless they's hot 'n fresh outta the oven!" An old man with a long thin wisp of a beard and a tattered misshapen straw cowboy hat barreled through the back door and slammed an armful of logs on the floor next to the stove. He sat in a big wooden chair at the head of the table, tucked a towel under his chin and started heaping food on his plate. "Come on boys, dig in!" And dig they did.

The trio ate in silence enthusiastically devouring all their favorite foods as the young girl, probably about eight years old, sat in a chair on the other side of the stove contentedly playing with a handmade kachina doll. Terry was unable to tell if she was Indian or White, but he was certain she was some kind of an angel.

Terry's favorite food was fried chicken legs and there were plenty of them. Broken wing enjoyed a virtually unlimited supply of fry bread, beans, corn and peppers while the Old Man ate from a plate of huge soft pretzels swimming in yellow mustard. Dessert was different for each of them. Broken Wing ate spoonfuls of hot sweet rice simmered with sugar and raisins and garnished with cinnamon. Terry picked up a perfectly formed chocolate/vanilla twist cone that twirled to a peak almost a foot tall and licked voraciously. The Old Man guzzled three or four cans of ice-cold orange soda.

As Terry got down to the cone part, he stopped licking and gazed abstractly at the long tunnels along the sides of the cone filled with melted ice cream. The best part always seemed to be sucking the creamy ambrosia out of the cone all the way to the bottom. He thought about that for a minute and realized he probably had not even had a cone like this since he was an adolescent, yet it was so familiar, and he was eating it as if it was something he did all the time. He and John used to ride their 20" bicycles a whole eight blocks, almost a mile, to Capitol Drive just to get one of these soft serve cones at Kitt's Drive-in; or they would go to Capitol Court, the third largest shopping center in the country, and venture up and down the various emergency staircases at Schuster's Department store chasing between racks of clothing on every floor to the next staircase door until they came out in the basement at the little cafe that served the same delicious treat. Terry seldom had enough money to buy one but John, who received a weekly allowance, would usually be able to afford one for each of them.

"Yep, Terry, them ol' days sure were fun, eh? You guys sure blew off a lotta steam on yer adventures in ice cream cones. Heh, heh, 'Adventures in Ice Cream Cones!' That'd make a great kid's book, eh Terry!?"

Terry snapped out of his reverie and looked quizzically at the Old Man who had just spoken as if he were reading Terry's mind. Just as quickly, doubt left him, and he went back to his cone and took the last crunchy bite into his mouth and savored the remaining bit of ice cream that went with it. He sat back in contentment with not a worry or care in the world. He was amazingly alert and quite aware of his surroundings and the people he was with. It seemed so natural and normal, as if he were having dinner on any average day in the life of living in a forest on a mountain above the high desert with his family. It did not even occur to him how radically different his attitude and demeanor were from what they had been yesterday.

"Don't you want something to eat little girl?" Terry called over to the embodiment of what now looked clearly like a young Navajo girl with long black straight hair.

She looked up into his eyes with such a glow of love that Terry almost looked away it was so intensely beautiful.

"Ya see, Terry, love ain't somethin' ya have to grab fer or try ta make happen. It just is. Ain't it beautiful."

The Old Man paused for a moment, his face changed to a more serious demeanor and he spoke again in his articulate lawyer voice.

"Everyone has the ability to take care of themselves. We don't need each other to fix each other. Each person makes their own reparations, masters their own fears and provides for themselves everything they need and more. For, once in the glow of truth, infinity comes forth from the individual and spreads to all who would receive it. It is no longer me helping you or you helping her, it is infinity pouring itself out in complete abundance showing forth all that is good. We are all helping each other equally and simultaneously." The Old Man chuckled in his geezer voice. "Ain't that a pip, Terry!?"

Terry basked in the sunshine of complete wholeness. It was more than a feeling, more than just a great burden being lifted from him. It was even more than anything he had ever thought Utopia could be like. The little girl came to him and sat in his lap. "I love you Daddy", she said, and he gave her the biggest hug he had ever given.

Chapter Two: John's First Awakening

"You know, if I didn't know any better, I'd say we just traveled back to the 1950's and met some important guy early in his career about to make some big discovery," John mused not really expecting an answer as he was getting used to the Old Man's cryptic ways.

"Maybe ya' don't know any better, Johnny." quipped the Old Man. "Ya' jes' can't take time too seriously. You may think it's serious, all them deadlines 'n everything, but it really ain't nothin', nothin' at all."

"Hey, that's the first time you answered my direct question, even if I don't understand what you mean," John said disconcertedly, but very quickly his mind calmed down and he perused the beautiful landscape. He had always loved the mountains and the desert but had never been in this area before. The desert they had been traveling across had changed from prickly pear, ocotillo and tumble weeds to sparsely scattered Pinyon trees and white spruce with some patches of grass. They were leaving the harsh rocky desert behind and moving up mountains that were forested with tall pines and a more temperate climate. There was no road or highway to follow, yet the way was smooth with not a bump or rock in their path. John thought this was amazing, but not disturbing. Somehow it seemed normal and natural as if the land was paving itself just for them. Ahead the mountains were dark green with a sprinkling of white on the highest peak.

"That's the Chuskas, Johnny, named by the Navajo from their word, choosh'gai. Means 'white-colored spruce trees'." The Old Man's voice changed to the narrator of some kind of documentary. "To the Navajo the Chuska Mountains are a sacred male deity whose forests provide timber and whose grassy flanks provide grazing land for their many flocks of sheep. There are many green valleys below such as Canyon De Chelly where family clans live and grow their own food including a surplus they can sell in the city. Traditionally they traded at trading posts run by the white man whom they considered a necessary evil they could not entirely expel from their land."

"So what's so special about the Chuskas for us, Old Man?"

"They's not only sacred, they say strange goins' on are happenin' all the time, 'specially in the summer. You ever seen anything strange Johnny, like somethin' ya' jus' can't explain away?"

"You mean besides you? No, I don't think so."

"What about that time you were lost in the swamp when you were a teenager, or when you were a little kid sweeping the basement?"

"Huh!? What are you talking about?" John knew exactly what the Old Man was referencing for those two different moments had something very much in common which he could not explain but left an indelible impression on his mind. Along with the odd sense that someone or some entity had been with him at those moments came a sense of specialness, like having a secret invisible friend that was only for you and no one else could ever know. He had not actually seen anyone either time, but in his heart, he was sure someone had been there. When he was lost in the swamp, it was like an angel had helped him find his way back to the road. But in the basement when he thought he saw something disappear behind the furnaces he did not *think* he was in trouble; he simply did not realize the extent to which he was emotionally neglected and abused by his parents and how much he needed comfort and nurturing. When he was seven, he believed his family life to be normal and he assumed everyone lived the way they did: Dad was gone working most of the time. Of course, after his parent's divorce, he learned his Dad did far more than work when he was gone. He was out drinking, womanizing and gambling.

Mom always hid it from the rest of the family. Mom's daily hysterics always included screaming, calling him names and slapping him repeatedly for something as insignificant as muddy shoes. He had no idea what nurturing or emotional intimacy was because he had never experienced either one, except once when he was on a rare family trip with Terry's family:

They were camping out on some land Terry's Dad owned in northern Wisconsin. John was used to being away from his family in summer, but it was either YMCA summer camp or visiting his grandparents farm. This campout with Terry's family was a special treat. Terry and John got to sleep in a tent together and the rest of the family slept in a trailer. On the first evening, Terry and John were playing with water pistols. It started out friendly enough, just squirting water at each other. But things escalated. Moving up from the squirt gun, John got a glass of water and threw it at Terry. Feeling like he had gotten the last word, John squatted at the campfire and poked at it with a stick. "Hey, Johnny!" came a shout from behind and John turned to see Terry with a big grin on his face about to throw a bucket of water on him. John, hot stick in hand, jumped up and ran, but his short stocky legs could not out run Terry's lean muscular frame, so he thought quickly and slammed his back against the screen door of the trailer. *Terry won't throw the water now,* he thought, *it would get all over the inside of the trailer.* But Terry was so focused on throwing that bucket of water he did not think about the screen door, only his nemesis, arms stretched out across the trailer providing a perfect target. Terry emptied the pail of the water on him and ran. As the ice-cold water hit him, John's animal instinct took over and the smoking stick he was holding went flying out of his hand and smacked Terry right in the middle of his bare back as he was running past the campfire. Terry screamed and John was horrified. In that moment, he realized he had not meant to hurt his best friend, but animal instincts were in high play and his flight instinct sent him running off into the tall grass to hide.

After what seemed like an eternity, John heard Terry's Mom and two little sisters calling for him to come out. No way was he going to come out, he would be *murdered.* But Terry's Mom kept calling in such a sweet voice that he finally came out with his head down, knowing he was probably going to be slapped silly for what he'd done. Instead, Terry's Mom grabbed him and hugged him hard and would not let him go. She spoke soft words of comfort saying she knew he did not mean it and that they all loved him. John felt awkward in her grasp as nothing like this had ever happened to him before. He was not accustomed to being hugged and comforted. And love? No one ever said that word around his house.

He instinctively expected to be screamed at and called names while being slapped like his own Mom would do. This left him with unresolved feelings of unpunished guilt. But there was no guilt-trip being laid on him. He did not like all this compassion. It felt way too odd and unfamiliar. He wanted to go home to his Mom.

He and Terry went back to their tent, and Terry kept reminding him he had hit him with a burning stick while John kept telling Terry he did not mean it, and it was not burning it was only smoking a little from the fire. Terry's injury was not serious but, the next morning, John woke up with a feeling he had never experienced before. He was homesick. He was sub-consciously needing the punishment he should have received, and consciously longing for the familiarity of home and Mom. He spent the next three days staying in the tent crying. Terry tried to get him to come out and do things to little avail. They did go on Terry's uncle's milk route one day, but John just kept leaning out the truck window tears streaming down his face longing to be home. The memory of Terry's scream when the stick hit him was a horror that left him with a deep hole in the pit of his stomach and reminded him of how depressed and lonely he felt inside. Although the incident itself was not monumental, it triggered repressed emotions. He was terrified of abandonment, a feeling he developed through neglect by his

Father and condemnation from his Mom. He had been afraid he would lose Terry's friendship, a friendship he vitally depended on for emotional comfort, something he got very little of at home.

"Hey, Johnny, look out there. See that mountain peak on the left, and the other two on the right with that space in between?" John looked up with a start. "That there is one a' them uranium mines where they sent the Navajo in to work. Course the workers didn't know nothin' 'bout radiation 'n all but the oil companies and the Bureau of Atomic Energy sure did. The first ghosts began to appear from the 'red lungs' back in 1955. Leetso, the yellow monster they called it. Killed more Navajo and their families than the American and Spanish soldiers did. Poisoned the land, the water, the livestock and the very mud they built their homes with. Even now the radiation is still killin' people. I used ta spend a lot of time tendin' to all those lost minds. Not the dead folk, they's jus' fine, but the minds of greed and lust for power behind the whole schlamega. Hey ya' wanna see somethin' funny? Look above them two mountains."

John saw a small cloud above the mountains, white and puffy like cotton against a royal blue sky. "That's just a cloud Old Man. What's the big deal?"

"Keep 'a lookin' Johnny, yer gonna really see sumthin'."

John reluctantly looked back at the cloud and as he watched, it started to expand horizontally. It turned from white to silver/gray and shimmered like it was sprinkled with silver glitter. It expanded to hover over the entire visible mountain range and a column of its substance came down like a pillar of energy flowing into the mountains. As it touched the Earth's surface, rays of the silver cloud-energy shot out in all directions. One of the rays headed straight for them. John stood frozen, white as a ghost. Just before it reached him, it disappeared. The cloud above the mountain had resumed its original lazy shape and John's heart was pounding.

"I thought you were ready for it," the Old Man said in a new voice, "but you have not felt the full brunt of your hurt enough to be willing to release it. Your time will come soon. As soon as you discover that this life you are leading is not working simply because you have held on to its pains and its pleasures. You have tried so hard to be a good person, but you keep dabbling in things that you cannot control. Look at yourself, John Whitlock, look in the mirror. What do you see? Is it beautiful or is it ugly? Look hard and long. It will look ugly at first but soon you will see the beauty deep inside. Deep inside you now, you think of yourself as worm-slime, lower than the lowest and filthiest of all beings. You have tried and failed innumerable times to measure up to feeling worthy. You give up each time because you are paralyzed by fear. Fear of failure, fear of abandonment, fear of rejection, fear of punishment. These fears have been the basis for all your decisions. You were neither taught nor given any other basis for living.

"There is another way and it is inside of you. Only you can discover it and you will when you are ready to face and release your fears. The real substance of your life can be summed up in one word: goodness. You already are made up of good. Goodness is your very nature. It is your inheritance. You were born with it. You are worthy and have always been worthy of being on this planet. You do belong and you do have a great purpose, a purpose that is better than anything you could ever dream of even in your wildest imagination. You just do not know it yet.

"I have seen the greatest horrors history has conjured up. I have looked through them into their deepest center. At the core of everything I have seen pure gold shining in its fullness. And it is always there, wherever I look, in whomever I see, in whatever circumstance presents itself before me. You, too, shall see all these things and even more. The world and its people, in timeless struggle, will be shown their true nature by your example and mine. What appears as war shall become peace. What appears as sickness will be completely healed. What appears as lack will become infinite supply of everything. This wholeness shall appear as you and as those who are ready to join with you. Eventually you will see this wholeness in everyone, in everything, everywhere."

John was standing with tears streaming down his face. The Old Man had summed up his fears as if he had been there all along. He thought of how afraid he was of being hurt when he got home from playing; of the many times his Dad did not show up, leaving him feeling lonely and abandoned; of how afraid he had always been of making mistakes. He had been a perfectionist who could not live up to his own standards, standards that were so high he could see no end to them. He felt alienated and different from everyone else and longed to be special and unique so people would notice him. He thought of all the visions of fame and fortune that turned into lost years of drinking and cheating and neglecting his wife and child and how it led him to the depths of drunkenness and despair destroying his family, his job and his very sanity. Was he insane right now? What was happening to his battered and blistered ego? Had it burned up in the desert?

John fell to his knees.

He closed his eyes and saw a cloud of shimmering energy like the one he had seen moments ago filling the entire sky. It flowed down in a column into the top of the Old Man's head out his chest and into John's heart. It then flowed out of the top of his head and into the cloud. He saw the energy flowing both ways simultaneously in a circular flow that somehow seemed to encompass all the land and sky around them. He saw that is was covering the entire Earth, the Solar system and the whole Universe and it filled him with immense joy and peace.

He knelt basking in this peace for quite a while. He opened his eyes and the landscape was back to normal. The cloud was gone, but he felt different. "Is this what God is?"

"Not God, John, not the way most people think of God. It's the one substance that makes up everything and everyone: the substance of all goodness and pure love. Some call it pure consciousness and it is the reality of all things."

"I...I feel something, something strange, like maybe it's all going to be alright somehow."

"That's called hope. You have always had it although you have seldom felt it. You are beginning to realize it. Hope comes as a feeling at first, then blossoms into belief in

yourself. Fear dissipates in its presence. Illness, poverty, depression and guilt all disappear. When the time comes, you will tap into this new consciousness and find there is power that will change many lives."

John's gaze was far off, as if he were looking into and beyond the past and the future, into the present. "You know I would drink always trying to find some solace, some peace from my fears and to numb my overwhelming sense of guilt. Now it's gone. The desire to drink - all gone!" John chuckled. "Hey, am I allowed to feel this good! Wow! This is amazing! You are amazing! Thanks, Old Man!"

"Ya' did it, Johnny. Ya' took the first step!"

John's chuckle turned into a laugh and the Old Man laughed along with him, took him by the hands and started dancing a jig. John felt so clean, so sober and so excited that he kicked up his feet and danced around and around with the Old Man. They danced past sunset and all through the night and did not stop until the next morning.

Chapter Three: The Reunion

Terry stood and watched as Broken Wing drove down the mountainside toward his home. He had no doubt that Broken Wing would find a way back into his clan and do plenty of good, because the change in him was permanent, and he carried an ever-glowing presence of love wherever he went. His people would notice this, for sure. He felt comfort and peace inside, not because of anything Broken Wing had said or done, not because of the Old Man or the strange little girl. But simply because of what he discovered inside his own heart. He had become conscious of the perfect harmony within himself. He really was a beautiful person after all. Those nasty things his Father had done were not his legacy. They had disappeared into a mist of forgiveness. Inside he felt full to overflowing and longed only to let it pour out to the whole world.

Terry had lost track of time and did not know how many days they had been on this mountainside, but each day delicious meals were provided and each day he felt at peace and at home. Few words were exchanged between the four. Terry spent a lot of time sitting on a rock gazing at the tall trees. He watched the woodpeckers tap their beautiful song of abundance as they searched for breakfast in the tree bark.

He would lie on the ground looking at white puffy clouds floating lazily across the azure sky.

On one of those days, Broken Wing had gone to his truck, about three miles downhill, dragging an axle the Old Man told him to take off the dune buggy. He said he hadn't used it in years anyway and a new means of transportation would always be available when it was needed. Broken Wing had protested that there was no way that axle would fit his truck but, sure enough, when he returned driving his truck, he said it not only fit perfectly, but the job went quite smoothly.

The little girl was still a puzzle to Terry. He had never married, never had a child, in fact he seldom had relations with the opposite sex as he was entirely consumed with staying high at all times. Yet he never thought to ask her anything about herself. He simply enjoyed her company and accepted her calling him Daddy. He often assisted with preparing the meals. She would tell him where the flour was or the meat or the vegetables and he would open a cupboard door and, like magic, what she asked for was there. Every day it was different. If he had thought about it, he would have realized not only was there not enough space for all the food he pulled out, but the food should not be so fresh and ready to prepare like it had just come from the grocery store.

So, the necessities of everyday living were always provided in this new way of life with no effort on his part except to show up to use and enjoy them. He felt it perfectly fine to sit and contemplate the beauty and the beautiful people surrounding him for hours on end. He often lost track of the Old Man who seemed to disappear sporadically to who knows where. But like clockwork, he always appeared through the back door of the cabin at meal time dropping another armful of firewood next to the stove.

As the last cloud of dust from Broken Wing's truck disappeared in the distance the Old Man appeared behind Terry and said, "It's almost time."

"I understand,' said Terry and although he had no idea what to expect next, he completely accepted and trusted his fate. He did know that whatever would come his way was not to be feared, judged or condemned. He somehow knew in his heart that the adventure was only beginning and soon, very soon, wonderful things would be happening for many others besides himself.

Terry followed the Old Man up the mountainside behind the cabin until they reached a ridge where they could see to the east for quite a few miles. A hawk flew overhead and shrieked. Several black crows were chasing it and chattering away declaring their territory. The wind was mild and warm and had a slight scent of juniper. Far in the distance amidst the tall pines was a tiny cloud of dust that trailed off to the east. The head of the cloud was coming their way and Terry's interest piqued. The thought of Federal Agents popped into his mind but was quickly supplanted by that warm safety and comfort he felt inside. There was nothing to fear. There would never again be anything to fear. There will always be a good way to handle any possible contingency and he trusted completely in this revelation. No matter who or what was coming, he was ready to face it with confidence.

Now he could hear the roar of an engine embedded with unintelligible shouts that sounded like men having a really great time. He turned to the Old Man and saw he had disappeared. He looked east again to see a dune buggy coming quickly up the slope driven by an old man with a bushy white beard and tattered straw cowboy hat. *Could it be,* he thought? Beside him was a younger man who looked somewhat familiar. They were singing, or more like shouting, an old rock tune: "Smoke on the wa-a-a-ter, da, da, da, da, da, dada, da, da, da, dada!"

The dune buggy came sliding sideways to a halt in front of him and the two men stepped out through a cloud of dust.

"Yep, it's who ya' think it is." The Old Man looked crossways at Terry and John. "Come one boys, time fer a big ol' hug!"

John came to a halt in front of Terry, looked into his eyes and shouted, "Terry! Terry! It's you!" and they hugged on queue as the Old Man waved his arms like he was directing a symphony and the choir sang:

"They have become the expression of good,
Good shining as good;
They have been lifted from pain and despair,
As they realize who they are.
The addictions disappear,
The addictions disappear.

Into the nothingness from where they came,
So goes all judgement, all guilt and all blame,
The addictions disappear;
The afflictions disappear.

On the path of enlightenment, especially when the path begins at the end of a trail of tears, the traveler is usually not disturbed by any surprising events or outward appearances. To him, all events are recognized as transitional experiences which are temporary and quite manageable taken one at a time in the present moment. This is how it was for Terry at the moment of his reunion with John. Perhaps it was because he had suffered so long and so hard, taking drugs and cough syrup for psychological and emotional survival rather than pleasure and enjoyment. Partly it may have been due to having seen and heard so many shocking things in his childhood, and all the horrors he saw as an often desperate addict and drug dealer. Moreover, he had lost everything and had virtually nothing more to lose. All his past seemed washed away in the last few days of peace and fulfillment, and this prepared him with the confidence and strength to face any new situation with unquestioning poise and dignity.

John on the other hand was filled with questions. He admittedly felt better physically and knew he was free of his alcohol addiction, and he had started to actually have fun traveling with the Old Man, but he was still confused and uncertain of his future. He wanted to know why he was here, where were his wife and child now, did he still have a job, what was going to happen to him, how was he going to get out of the mess he made of his life and so much more. He was still self-absorbed and concerned about himself and his fate. He had an underlying guilt and shame in spite of his miraculous recovery from alcoholism that kept him running ahead of himself to avoid those horrible feelings. He wanted to know why this strange Old Man had shown up, where he came from and what he was doing here. He wanted to learn how he could be meeting Terry in the most unlikely of places and how he could so completely lose his desire to drink and actually be happy about it. Terry, on the other hand, had not a single thought concerning his own fate. He was filled with peace and joy beyond description. He had no desire to know why anything was happening. He was willing to accept and deal with anything that came up, always trusting himself and the goodness of the universe to be there. He had no wants or needs other than embracing the moment in pure light and love. And he was ready for action.

"Terry...Terry...how *are* you?" The question sounded foolish and trite to John, but he really didn't know what to say. Terry's countenance was serene, and he waited for the Old Man to speak.

The Old Man, standing on a large rock, gazed beyond their sight and began. "The time has come for you to come together and resume the battles you fought as little boys with stick guns against invisible armies. Terry, the peace that has come over you is a powerful weapon against those armies, more powerful than an atom bomb yet as harmless as a stick-gun. With a simple gesture of the hand, peace, harmony and love will pour forth to those you meet. This is your gift given for you and for all. It will turn hatred into love, discord into harmony, sadness into joy, despair into hope.

Your mere presence will evoke peace, end arguments and dispel prejudices. It will be effortless on your part. You need only show up and do each task as presented in each moment. You will go unnoticed by many, but those who see you shall embrace your love and know goodness as they have never known. "

Terry remained still and looked unsurprised by these statements. John's mouth was hanging open and his eyes were big, his pupils like pinpoints. As often as he had heard the Old Man go into these articulate reveries, this one was different, like he was someone else, not even a person at all but a disembodied voice booming in a huge cavern. He wondered what all this had to do with him.

As if he had been reading his mind, the Old Man proclaimed, "John, you may ask your question now."

"You saved me from dying in the desert and I really thought all this time you were taking me back to civilization so I could try to put the pieces of my life back together. Now you take me to this mountain which, coincidentally is the home of my best childhood friend, and start endowing us with some mission I never even heard of and that, frankly, makes no sense at all. *'Resuming battles with stick guns?'* What? Are we supposed to start playing in the fields again?"

Terry's face changed and he looked warmly at John. "Hey, John. We had some great adventures when we were little didn't we? They don't seem like much now, but then it was us discovering new territories. The back stairwells at Schuster's Department Store were like portals to new lands. We traversed many stairs and stepped through each door into a new department that was, to us, an undiscovered continent or planet that we could explore for a bit until we came to another portal and excitedly pushed it open into yet another brand new world. Do you remember how exciting those moments were?"

"Yes," replied John, "but that was all make believe."

"Are you sure?" Terry responded. "Maybe thinking the men's shoe department was a battle ground for superheroes was make believe, but what about the feeling you had? Wasn't it real? Wasn't it like the feelings you've been having with the Old Man after you saw the cloud? Like you've gone through a portal and are in a strange new land ready to fight an invisible army?"

"There you go with that invisible army stuff - Hey! How'd you know about the cloud? Could you see it from here?"

"Yes, I see it from here. I see it now. It is everywhere, surrounding us, flowing through us, in and out of our heads and hearts and it seems to have no beginning and no ending. It is radiating everywhere."

"That's were yer wrong Terry. It has a beginning. Right ch'ere," and the Old Man pointed to Terry's heart, then to John's heart, then to his own. "And that's the only place it kin start. Everybody's got it. Ya' jus' have ta' push the right button to git it a' goin.'"

"I saw it yesterday," John replied, "and I sure felt good afterwards. I'm ashamed to tell you I became a drunk, an alcoholic, hopelessly addicted and I hurt a lot of people. But as of yesterday, I have no desire to drink! Not even a little bit!" He looked sheepishly at the Old Man. "And, well, we did sort of dance together."

Terry laughed. "Trust me. I know all about dancing and singing and even playing the flute."

"I've been so happy since then,' continued John, "having fun driving and singing, making up funny stories, laughing at those funny jack rabbits and roadrunners skittering across our path. And I sure do remember how amazing that cloud was, but I don't see it now."

"Well trust me, John," said Terry, "it is here and very real. You remember what a druggie I was. Well, it got worse, much worse until I had to run away. I could have spent the rest of my life in Federal Prison. Only a few days ago all my cravings were lifted. Completely gone. But it was so much more than that. I literally stumbled into a peace and joy so wonderful that I know I will never have to go back to the old ways. Now I am living the even older ways: the ways the Ancient Ones speak of as the connection to the Spirit of Mother Earth. These ways are the instructions for nurturing our planet and caring for each other with respect by being mindful of the sacredness of all things. These ways have been revealed to me the last few days and are unfolding for you. It is the consciousness that everyone and everything is made of Spirit, and that Spirit is infinite goodness. I didn't know these things a few days ago, but now I am certain that I was only blind to them for they have always existed. I was searching for peace by trying to blot out the pain of the past and the fear of the future with drugs. It turned out to be oblivion, not peace, and I was getting into more and more trouble until my big grandstand attempt to run away, just like you tried to run away from your troubles."

"I was thrown off a train in the middle of the desert! I was in a blackout. I didn't run away!"

"Yeah, right! Your drinking had nothing to do with it!" Terry and the Old Man shouted in unison. They chuckled. Their chuckles built into laughter. Their laughter crescendoed until John could not help but laugh with them. The Old Man fell on the ground his arms and legs flailing in the air like a happy baby. Terry and John grabbed each other and held on tight as if their laughter was going to lift them off the ground and propel them into the sky.

Through sobbing chuckles John finally said, "Oh I get it now. My drinking caused me to be thrown into the desert. All these years I've been running away from my troubles by drowning them in booze!" and he fell to his knees as his laughter turned to grief. With no alcohol to cover it up, his psychological wall of protection gave in and the pain of his past flowed out in a stream of fresh tears. Like a flash flood from a mountain that had been holding back the waters and could no longer take the strain, his tears burst forward. He felt like his emotions were being bashed against the rocks and torturing him inside and out. The unsuppressed guilt and shame came out in waves, and with each one, he sobbed harder. But, just as the waters push the rocks down the mountainside cleaning and smoothing them, years of suppressed pain and guilt were being washed away and, with each wave of grief, he felt cleaner, lighter and more alive.

Terry and the Old Man put a hand on John's shoulder and patiently stood by letting John's grief runs its course. After a while, John stood, squeezed their hands and smiled through his subsiding tears.

"Thank you...thank you...thanks for being here with me. Thank you for your kindness. Thank you! Thank you! Thank you!

"Well he's a gittin' somewheres, eh Terry?"

"Yep, he shore is!" chimed Terry.

Chapter Four: Sadoval the Navajo

John Whitlock had always thought of himself as a visionary, a dreamer, a creative artist whose potential was suppressed by the demands of others. Employers, clients, family, friends and anyone he perceived as an authority figure misunderstood him and held him back from realizing his full potential. Sure, he had colleagues and friends he could work and play with shoulder to shoulder, but he spent most of his energy trying to be what he thought they expected him to be so they would accept him, and, on his deepest level, so they would not hurt him like his parents had. What he thought was other people keeping him from fulfilling life's dreams, was his own self so busy trying to arrange people so he could be safe and happy. Because he did not have the satisfaction of developing his true desires, he needed some kind of support from the outside to make him feel at least a little bit worthy. So he thrived on the praise of others. He worked hard at earning that praise by trying to please them, and left his own visions, dreams and musical talents by the wayside. He manipulated people with kindness and graciousness so they would give him the thing he wanted most; the thing he could not find within himself: a sense of worthiness.

His deep-set feelings of inferiority and guilt eventually led him to act out the part of the outcast who would never amount to anything. When he did bad things, like getting drunk and philandering, it actually seemed to temporarily settle the dispute in his mind and convince him that, yes, he was lower than worm slime. Didn't his actions prove this?

Yet none of these things had ever before risen to the level of his conscious mind with the exception of temporary moments of shame that he quickly suppressed with alcohol, sex, work or other distractions. This day with Terry and the Old Man became his moment of truth, the moment he faced himself and could clearly see who he had been, how he had been thinking and the true nature of the way he had been living. Simultaneously, with this burgeoning awareness of his defects, came an awareness of an incredibly beautiful, loving presence inside himself that was flowering like a beautiful orchid out of a garbage pit. This presence gave him strength and courage to look at his life more objectively. And it came with a sense of hope that he would somehow be able to make reparations and become a source of good for his loved ones.

"Ain't so ugly ta look at when ya' know what yer made of, eh Johnny boy?" the Old Man said in his usual mind-reading way. John didn't really think the Old Man read minds, yet he sensed a connection so strong with him that it no longer surprised him when the Old Man responded as if he did.

John felt as light as a feather like he could float up into the sky. He opened his arms wide embracing the mountains and sky and felt at peace. He looked over at Terry.

"So, Terry...so...exactly what are we doing out here? Aren't things just a little bit peculiar to you?"

Terry looked at John with clear eyes and a bright countenance and simply said, "We are here now."

Before John could even sort that one out enough to think of what to say next the Old Man interrupted. "Now listen boys, enough about you. It is time to put this here radiating energy into action. We got a whole lot ta' do."

John looked anxiously at the Old Man. "Shouldn't I be getting back to my family? I have a lot of-"

"In time, Johnny, all in *good* time. Follow me."

Terry started immediately behind the Old Man as he began to descend the eastern slope of the mountain. John was again confused but not so much by the Old Man as by the fact that he did not hesitate to follow both of them without a word of protest. Questions like, 'Wouldn't it be easier to take the dune buggy?' or 'Shouldn't we stock up on water and food?' crossed his mind but left it as fast as they came. Instead, John watched his feet as they took one step at a time down what was clearly a gravel path. He noticed the sunlight shining on the gravel causing sparkles that seemed to flicker on and off as he walked. He squatted down and picked up a few pebbles and held them in the palm of his hand. They were multi-colored: silvers, pinks, reds, greens grays and yellows. They glittered in the sunlight. He was amazed at how beautiful a few simple pieces of gravel could be when you take the time to stop and notice. He thought of nothing but the pebbles as he set them gently back on the path and looked up. Terry and the Old Man were nowhere in sight.

"Hey Terry! Old Man! Wait for me!" There was no response. He could see at least a half-mile down the path and there was not even a stirring of dust, not to the left or the right either. John stood and began walking forward. Immediately Terry was walking forward directly in front of him on the path following the Old Man. They seemed undisturbed as if they had been there all the time. Everything looked the same with one big difference, the sun was now behind them. It was late afternoon and only a moment ago it had been mid-morning! He thought it through and remembered the little trip they took through time to save that geologist and choose his words carefully.

"So... *when* are we now, Old Man?" John asked trying to sound as casual as possible.

"Sa-a-ay, Johnny, yer gettin' smarter. 'Course its yer second trip. This here is Terry's first, ya wanna fill him in?" the Old Man asked confidently as if John was in on some kind of plan.

"I don't know-"

"Aw jus' go ahead. The words'll come."

"Okay, I'll try. Some time yesterday we were driving through the flat desert when a cliff seemed to materialize in front of us and we saw a man trapped near the top on a ledge. We drove around to the top and rescued him with a rope I didn't even know we had. It turns out he was a geologist working for the Bureau of Atomic Energy sent to look for signs of Uranium. His name was William Maestro and he discovered uranium in the Chuska Mountains over sixty years ago!"

John paused to let that sink in expecting Terry to be surprised.

Instead Terry spoke nonchalantly over his shoulder. "That would make sense seeing as time is simply a man-made construct. We have the three dimensions of space which we have learned to move around in quite well. When we see time as simply the fourth dimension, we should be able to move through it just like we can move physically in any of the three physical dimensions."

"Huh?" replied John.

"We are only limited by our own belief in our limitations. The Universe is unlimited. Tap into that and anything is possible."

"You know, Terry, your sisters didn't call you 'the brain' for nothing. But anyway, that cliff did not materialize, we just moved in time and space back to 1950 apparently to save this guy. Hey! I said that like it was no big deal defying all the know laws of physics! Then we drove off and he disappeared. Just now we moved into another time, I'm not sure when. I think we're in the same area where we met but I didn't see that pass up ahead before. Let's see, we're still on the same mountain. The weather's changed a bit. It's a little cooler-"

John stopped abruptly. "Look, down in that pass! You see all the dust? You hear voices or shouting or something?" Just then what looked like a Native American came galloping up the slope on a very handsome pinto pony brandishing a spear and shouting. As he was almost upon them, Terry raised his left hand to about shoulder level palm up and blew across it toward the horseman, the Old Man said, "Ya-te-hey," and the young rider and his black and white steed came to an abrupt halt in front of them and replied quite calmly, "Ya-te-hey."

John was startled for only a moment as he was getting used to just about anything happening around the Old Man. He thought he had seen Terry blow a stream of a gray cloud-like substance off his hand toward the Native, but he dismissed it and studied this out-of-time looking stranger in front of him. The horseman was wearing thick fur of some kind and moccasins laced up to his knees. There was a leather saddle on the horse that was clearly embossed with 'U.S. Cavalry.'

"So you did steal that horse from the cavalry after all, eh Sadoval?" mused Terry abstractly.

142

"They stole first!" scowled the native as he stood up in the saddle and pointed his spear at Terry. "How do you know my name!" Terry heard him clearly in English, but all John heard was a language he did not understand.

Terry lifted his palm and blew, and the stranger calmed down and sat back in the saddle. "Hmm, this really works. 'Course I knew it would," and Terry smiled and sat on a rock.

The Old man appeared to be serious, more serious than John had ever seen him. "Sadoval, you must hurry. There is a cabin on the western slope of this mountain. Go there. You will find food, shelter, everything you need. Go there and wait. You will wait many seasons until you are an old man and you will think you are done but it is then that your people will need you the most. Go now! Hurry! There is a young squaw there who will be your partner for a long time. Do not worry about the cavalry. We will send them away."

John watched Sadoval closely as the Old Man spoke. He was still in the saddle, eyes fixed intently on the Old Man. After the Old Man spoke, Sadoval said something in his native tongue and took off in a gallop up the mountain to the west.

"So did that guy really understand what you said?" asked John. "I mean you were speaking English and all he spoke was, uh, what was he speaking anyway?"

"Navajo. He heard me in his own language." The Old Man looked over at Terry. "Thanks Terry boy I couldn't 'a done it without ya."

John was confused. "Who is this Sadoval anyway? And how did you know-"

"Cavalry's coming," Terry interrupted like he had been expecting them. John looked at a cloud of dust coming toward them from down in the pass.

"OK, Johnny it's yer turn." The Old Man gave John a push forward forcing him to run so he would not stumble down the steep incline.

In his mind, John thought he should be objecting, asking questions and getting some answers about all this. Yet in his heart he felt a strong sense of a confidence. His instincts to trust the Old Man took over and he responded with complete spontaneity. He found himself running down the mountainside waving his arms, pointing to the south and frantically calling out to the oncoming soldiers, "Hey! He went that-a-way! He went that-a-way!"

Chapter Five: The Plan

"He went that-a-way," Terry said sardonically to John. "Is that the best you could come up with?" he smiled.

"Well the Old Man didn't give me any time to think and I knew I had to put them off Sadoval's trail. Won't someone tell me who Sadoval is?" The Old Man responded by stirring the campfire with a stick and John watched the sparks float upward from the yellow flames. They seemed to change from orange to white and become the myriad of stars in the night sky. He gazed peacefully at the display of lights. It had been quite a day: abrupt changes, surprise meetings, unusual events. He was beginning to accept at least a little bit that all this made sense and worked out somehow, but he still had many questions.

Yet those thoughts were secondary to this new feeling that was welling up inside him. It was a feeling he had never experienced before, and it felt so good that he temporarily forgot his concern about the facts. He was more comfortable sitting around the campfire with Terry and the Old Man than he had ever been in his life. His heart was bouncing with joy and his stomach was filled with the soft sweet nectar of peace. He thought of the feeling he used to get when he took the first drink before it turned into the inevitable roaring drunk. It was hot going down, but in a few minutes, his stomach felt warm and comfortable and his heart was calm. The alcohol gave him fleeting moments of feeling comfortable in his own skin. Temporarily he felt like he did measure up to the world's standards. He felt like he belonged. He was artificially gratified. The problem was he wanted to keep that feeling and the only way he knew to get it was to drink. But the second and third and fourth drinks never worked as well as the first, but in his alcoholic insanity, he kept drinking until he was so drunk that he would make a fool of himself in public and do things he would not normally do like stealing, cheating on his wife, throwing up, and passing out and often waking up in a strange place with a woman he didn't recognize. Here with these friends he knew he was whole and complete. As long as he was in their presence, he knew he belonged to the human race and could hold his head up as a worthwhile contributing member. If he could stay around this campfire with the Old Man and Terry for the rest of his life, he would be perfectly happy.

"Yep, when you was skeedaddlin' down that mountain, Terry 'n me was laughin' so hard we could hardly see ya down there." said the Old Man. "Ya' see Johnny, all ya' gotta do is show up in the right place at the right time. You'll always know what ta' do next. Like fer instance..." He reached behind into the darkness and pulled out an acoustic guitar.

John froze as the Old Man held it out to him. He had not touched a guitar in years. He slowly reached out, took the guitar and set it on his lap. His eyes glazed as he stared right through it. His old hopes and dreams of becoming a famous musician flashed through his mind: his first wife, how he had done the worst thing anyone could ever do and ran way, abandoning her, his friends, his band and his life as a musician. The guitar was like hot lead pressing down on his thighs. He did not want to think about that now. He just wanted to die. He touched the neck with his index finger as if it were going to burn him. It almost surprised him that the neck felt normal, familiar and quite comfortable. He took it expertly into his hands, positioned it in classical style and gently plucked the 'A' string. The vibration of the note was almost imperceptible, but he could feel it resonating from the body of the guitar into his chest. He plucked it again. The sound moved through him until his whole body felt like it was vibrating an 'A'. Waves of sound radiated from his body like the ripples from a pebble dropped into a glassy pond flowing out in circles. He could see the Old Man and Terry, mouths open, taking a slow inhalation like they were tasting sweet nectar that rolled over their tongue and into their very souls resonating their bodies in pure harmonious vibration.

John closed his eyes and hummed, his voice resonating in perfect harmony with this one tone that now seemed so ubiquitous as to encompass the entire world.   His fingers moved fluidly across the strings plucking harmonies he had never heard.   His humming, so subtle, so sweet, took the shape of a melody that rose beyond emotional response into a place inside him that could only be described as bliss. He continued playing smoothly without pause as his humming formed into words...

As the sparks float into the sky and dissolve into the stars,
So my heart opens up wide and radiates out to you.
Together we now share,
In perfect harmony.
As we float up into the sky and become one with the stars.

As the life and strength we possess cannot be contained,
So we now open a way and let the splendor come forth.
Together we are one,
In perfect harmony.
All the love we now behold belongs to everyone...
...comes from everyone
...everyone is one.

The three ghostly figures sat in timeless infinity around the campfire's glowing orange embers as they floated into the black canopy and disappeared into the blaze of stars. Words were no longer needed to communicate as they basked in this invisible glory that was more real than anything John had ever thought was reality. This glory was not only here and now in this place with these friends; but it was as if it had always been with him, with them, ever-present but unconscious, now revealed to his consciousness. To John, this was not some new kind of belief, it was the opening of a door to a soul that had always existed inside him, a door that he had just now effortlessly walked through to a place of infinite discovery, strength and supply. He now knew he was in a world that made sense, a world where he belonged and played an integral part forming, shaping and, most of all, loving everyone He met everywhere he went. But, deserting his wife and daughter-

The Old Man interrupted before John's morbid reverie could took hold. "*Now* you know the plan, Johnny, what we're doin' out here. Why ya' came 'n all that."

"Yes, I see it now. There is nothing in the outside world to seek in order to make my life make sense. I found nothing in the bottle, no revelations, no happiness, no peace. I tried over and over and over again to find something there, but I only ended up drunk, despondent and alone." John stood, clasped his hands to his heart center and opened his arms wide trying to point to everything at once. "It's all here! I'm a part of it! You're a part of it! Wow! And you, Old Man, you are making all this happen, aren't you?!" John had become dependent on the Old Man's presence to feel this sense of connection and unspeakable joy. From the start, the Old Man gave him clarity, confidence, healing and sobriety.

John asked, "We can go anywhere and do anything we want, can't we?"

And it was Terry who answered. He sat back on his elbows and said, "And it is now your choice how you are going to use it. You can choose to follow this bliss, or you can choose to go back to the pain and misery of your old life. It doesn't matter where you go or who you're with, it's an inside job. It's what you decide that makes the difference. You can choose to go back to your old ways, or you can choose the other side and remake your marriage, actually your entire life, into something beautiful that can be a shining light of good. You can choose this new way, the way of giving and loving always drawing upon an infinite supply of it from your very own soul which is connected to it whether you stay with us, go back to your family or move to Timbuktu!"

"Hee hee, Tim Buck Too, that's a good 'un, Terry but the way I heered it was..." and the Old Man's voice changed again, "The place you find yourself in at this moment is the place of peace and the place of purpose. Take note of your surroundings and the people you are with at this moment. This is where you belong now and where you will go next will be totally dependent on the choice you make now. Choose pain and misery by suffering in guilt and fear and guilt and fear will take you to the next place. Choose love, peace and harmony and these will take you to the next place. You see, you are not really choosing the next place you will go, you are choosing the attitude or paradigm that is the basis for taking you to the next place. It is *that* which dictates your next move. The actual physical move to different places, the changing of relationships, or getting new and better things does not cause any permanent change. It is the spirit in which you move at this moment that moves you to the next."

"So what'll it be, eh Johnny boy," Terry interjected, "back to your old life, or make a new one?"

"You mean I can change the future course of my life into something good choosing, what did you say, love, peace and harmony in the present moment? And with love as the basis for all my choices, I can rebuild my family and my career?"

"Not *rebuild*, John, *remake*. You can actually start over again," said Terry.

"Yer thinkin' too much Johnny. Play us a song now. Play that song you wrote 'bout choosin'," said the Old Man.

"I don't know..." and John gazed into the Old Man's eyes and, as if they were picture tubes, saw the image of himself about 10 years younger in his early twenties sitting in his living room recording studio playing his guitar and singing. He remembered the song he was writing at that time that went so deep he never really understood its meaning: The Choice. He closed his eyes and began finger-picking in Em. The words and music flowed out easily. As he sang each line, he breathed in its deeper meaning:

I am the human – the one that you seek
I am the satisfier – the one who made you weak
Too weak to tell the difference between yourself and my soul
Because of all you longed for and covered up so well
Too weak to find your convictions – the place where you must stand
Because your self was never good enough…self was never good enough…
Good enough for anyone to see.

I am the no man – the one you craved to see
I am the compensation for pain and misery
For I took you out and dined you every time that you asked
And swore you'd never hurt again, that this would always last
And because you knew not who you were I fooled you in the end
When you landed on your face…flat on your face…
Again and again.

I am the one man – the one that you sought
I am the pre-conceiver – the one with whom you fought
Because you wanted me and hated me for what you weren't inside
Your life was pain concealed, covered up with pride
So you've torn yourself to nothingness inside your paper bag
Until the only thing left…the only thing left…

The only thing left is to decide!!!

MAKE A DECISION! The choice is left to you.
MAKE A DECISION! The choice is left to you.

I am the enemy who took you to the pits
I am the destroyer who smashed your life to bits
Because you never would have seen that I am nothing in this scene
Except the advocate of alternatives that make you want to scream
So now it's up to you, it's time to decide
Choose your pain and misery or choose the other side
Now you know the difference, there's no reason left to hide:
The only thing left…the only thing left…
The only thing left is to decide!!!

MAKE A DECISION! The choice is left to you.
MAKE A DECISION! The choice is left to you.

After he had finished, he was certain which choice he would make and, in fact, realized he had already made it.

Chapter Six: Sadoval at the Diner

John Whitlock was lying in contemplation next to the still warming campfire in the early morning quiet after a good night's sleep. He mused only for a moment on how the fire could still be burning so well and how he stayed so warm and comfortable without a blanket, but provision of his physical needs seemed unimportant and almost taken for granted as his thoughts quickly turned to this moment and how it was he was even here at all. As the other two slept, he thought about these strange new feelings he was having. He was conscious of a new internal sense of a 'something' he could not wrap his mind around and define. He could describe it somewhat with adjectives like 'peace', 'contentment', 'well-being', 'goodness' and other words whose sum total still fell short of completely defining what it was that he could now see and feel.

He was coming to realize that Terry was in a more developed state consciousness of this 'something'. It showed in Terry's ability to take everything that happened in stride, no matter how crazily or suddenly things transpired, and in his method of calming down people with a simple hand-wave and a puff of breath. *And* the way he *knew* things like the Old Man knew things, things that usually didn't make sense to John. As for the Old Man, his constant confidence and trust in everything that was going on around them was an inspiration. Nothing seemed to ruffle the Old Man's feathers and he was able to fearlessly face and literally 'live in' the truth and often laugh with it. John could see that the Old Man lived in complete joy and it gave John a sense of trust in the way things were unfolding. What he did not yet fully realize was that what he could see in others, was also in him.

Guilt feelings surfaced again about his wife and child and destroyed the panacea of thoughts. Dear sweet Sarah. Oh how he missed his little girl. He felt so guilty about chastising her for leaving her trike in the driveway. He was the one who almost ran it over and felt especially guilty that it was really his fault, yet he blamed her. In his mind he clearly saw her in the bushes hugging her Teddy bear's ears and whimpering. *Oh, god how could I have been such a fool not to realize how precious and important she is, he thought.* No, all he thought of then was getting that first drink. Every muscle in his body screamed 'Drink!' 'Drink!' 'Drink!' and he stepped over everyone and everything just so he could bask in the temporary comfort of his bottle of booze. He did try hard to be nice and loving toward his family and good to his friends and co-workers. He really was a nice guy; but when push came to shove the alcohol was priority number one. Its double-edged sword was his salvation and his undoing.

John was settling into a good session of self-pity and morbid reflection when Terry awoke him from his reverie. "John, John, wake up. It's time to go through the next portal."

"The next what?"

"Aw, don't ya' worry yer head 'bout it Johnny. You hungry? How 'bout some bacon 'n eggs! Whaddaya say, boys!" The Old Man stood up, waved them forward and they stepped through the door of... an old-fashioned quaint cafe.

There were thirteen metal stools with round red cushioned tops and no backs lined up around an 'L' shaped counter with a laminated fake marble top. Behind the counter was a middle aged somewhat attractive waitress with bleached blond hair and a pony tail in a hairnet wearing a bright yellow bib apron.

"Coffee, boys?" the waitress said leaning up against the counter.

Terry and the Old Man spun their way onto stools leaving an empty one between them and the waitress, her red and yellow name tag said 'Peggy', slapped three cups down and poured the steaming hot brew from a glass coffee pot she took off the warming plate behind her. To the right of the coffee maker was a four-slot toaster, then two gas burners with an egg pan on one followed by a small hot grill with a shiny silver vent-a-hood above it. On the other side of the coffee was a stainless-steel milk dispenser with a thick round metal handle, and two soup warmers with ladle handles jutting out of two steel pots. On the end was a cooler with glass doors filled with pies, butter and cans of whipped cream.

John stood in jaw-gaping frozen silence fixated on this little scene then turned around and looked out the glass door they had just walked through. Instead of desert he saw a paved street with sidewalks and street lamps. Across the street was a storefront with an orange and blue sign that said, 'Rexall Drugstore'. He noticed a 1946 rusty faded green Desoto 4-door with fat whitewall tires pulling up to the curb just outside the door in front of a parking meter, an *analog* parking meter, the old-fashioned put-your-money-in-the-slot and turn the handle kind. A tall husky dark-skinned man with two long silver-gray braids and a cowboy hat slammed the car door and walked brusquely into the restaurant. As he walked past, John noticed deep creases in his bronzed face and the smell of old leather from his buckskin jacket. His jaw was square and set hard in his face in contrast to his deep black eyes which seemed to twinkle like LED lights in a marble bust. This man had the air of wisdom carved out of years of hard experience. John figured his age to be anywhere from forty-five to ninety-five. He was too robust to be ninety-five yet something about him looked very old indeed.

The man sat down at the end of the counter and Peggy brought him a cup of black coffee, a matchbox and a newspaper. He pulled out a pouch and a little packet of cigarette papers and expertly rolled a cigarette with one hand, licked it, jabbed it into his mouth and lit it with a wooden match. It had been so long since smoking had been allowed in restaurants that John almost spoke up but he quickly realized he was probably somewhere in the past, most likely even before smoking was said to cause cancer.

"Another one 'a yer people died from the yellow monster," Peggy said sympathetically. "Little article on page 7 there, sweetie." The man grunted and thumbed through the paper. John tried to look at the date on the front of the paper without being noticed but the paper was too wrinkled and when the man finally held it still, the corner was folded over so all he could make out was a huge headline that read, 'Uranium Boom Continues'.

"Ya' like yer coffee hot, don't cha Johnny?" said the Old Man.

"Uh, yeah," and John sat between his two friends and took a sip. He looked above the coffee maker at the large hand-painted menu. It was bright yellow with red lettering. There was only a dozen or so items on it. One read, 'Coffee 10 ¢'. John inhaled deeply and shook his head as he exhaled trying to clear the confusion from his mind. Pulling himself together a little he said, "I'll have ham and eggs, hash browns and whole wheat toast."

"We ain't got no hash browns, sweetie'. Only got white toast,' Peggy replied with a firm but friendly tone.

"Fine, Fine. You have any orange juice?"

"Nope. Just that orange drink over there." She pointed to the other end of the counter and John saw a vintage drink machine that consisted of a large rectangular clear plastic bowl with a bubbly bright orange liquid inside atop a one-glass dispenser.

"Woo wee! Orange soda! Gimme a big glass 'a that Peggy," the Old Man interrupted.

Just then two big husky white men walked through the door engaged in an intense conversation.

"Yeah them Indians sure got it made. They's all gittin' rich off that uranium," one man said.

"Sure, if not from the leases on their land, from the high wages they get workin' in them mines," the other replied.

"Sure wish I was in their shoes," said the first.

From behind his newspaper, the man in the braids said quite matter-of-factly, "If you were, you'd be sick or dying from radiation exposure."

The two men were just about sitting down when they heard this. They both stood up straight and the one who appeared to be the spokesman said, "What's that supposed to mean, injun!"

The other man took a step toward the Native American snarling his lips and pounding his fist in his palm. Terry, who seemed oblivious to what was happening as he calmly sipped his coffee lifted his hand slightly above his head while blowing over his coffee cup. Peggy interjected diplomatically, "Hank, Bob, what kin ah git you boys?"

"Oh, howdy Peggy," said the spokesman and the two men sat down quite contentedly at the other end of the counter seemingly forgetting about the Native American at the other end. "Two cups a' coffee and bacon 'n eggs fer both of us. Uh, make mine scrambled. Bob here'll have 'em sunny side up." Hank pulled a copy of the newspaper from his coat pocket.

"Hey, gimme the sports section," said Bob.

"Naw, I'm gonna read it. Here, you kin have the funnies!" Hank laughed and Bob joined in as if nothing had ever happened.

Meantime, on the other end of the counter the voice spoke again from behind the newspaper. "Old Man, you got something for me?"

"Let's go," said the Old Man.

"But what about my breakfast!?" protested John and he looked pleadingly over at Peggy who had not yet started to make the food. The Old Man slapped a dollar bill on the counter, and they walked out the door followed by the pigtailed stranger. Oddly, John felt as satisfied as if he had just eaten a huge breakfast.

This unlikely quartet got into the old Desoto parked out front with pig-tails in the driver seat, Terry next to him and John and the Old Man in the back seat. John noticed the town was small and, in a few minutes, they were passing by the last house and headed down a two-lane highway into the high desert. A signpost read, 'Thank you for visiting Grants, New Mexico,' and the highway sign denoted Route 66 West.

"Go ahead, Terry, it's your turn," said the Old Man and Terry lifted his hand to blow. "Naw, Terry, jus' tell Sadoval here the next move."

"So you're - I see," said Terry. "Well, Sadoval you've been waiting a long time for the Old Ones to come to you and tell you your purpose. I realize this is usually done in a sweat lodge with a sipapuni, that hole in the middle of the floor where the ancestors come out and speak their wisdom. But, well, we are here as you can see so we can dispense with the formalities."

"I have seen the ancestors take on many forms,' said Sadoval. "When we first met, I knew you were there to direct me, and the Old Man was the wise one, so I obeyed. And he was right. The young girl was my companion for many years, and we lived a good life on the mountainside. All our needs were met, and we were happy. When she went to the beyond, I was saddened yet joyful for this is our destiny and we only transform, we do not die. I spent the next decades studying the Medicine Ways as I remembered them, taught to me by my Grandmother when I was young. Many sweat lodges and much prayer revealed many things to me; but it never revealed what I was waiting for or when it would happen. I have always trusted the words of the Old Man for they were strong and true when he spoke. 'Wait, wait' he said, so I waited, and I am here now, and I am ready to help my people."

"Your people are dying in far greater numbers than anyone will ever know," Terry said. "The government and media keep it as quiet as they can, but we know. The Uranium mines are not only infecting the lungs of the workers, but the tailings are contaminating the water supplies and the air. So many men, women and children will die from cancer and birth defects as well as from 'leetso' the yellow monster. And most of the world will only think the Navajo are getting rich, when it is the government and big oil companies that are taking all the profits. The radiation contamination will be the third greatest in history, greater than 3-mile Island and almost as bad as Chernobyl and Fukushima in area and death toll."

"You speak of things I do not yet know. You are more than Old Ones, you are something else," said Sadoval.

"Hey, I'm just a guy who got lost in the desert," John said humbly from the back seat. His alcoholic ability to minimize a situation was still in full gear.

Terry continued, "You have had more years than anyone in all of history to learn the Medicine Way, and you can now practice better than any living man. Now it is time for you to sing the songs and perform the rituals for your people. You and I can see they are in trouble, but there is more to it than that. The Medicine Way is for you first, then for your people, then for all people. Your song shall go throughout the world silently and strongly and those who would hear shall receive its blessings and be changed. This change will move them from a fear-based life to the realization of the all-good Great Spirit that is in all people and ever-present, what your people call the Creator. They shall go on to live this new way of love and it will be the basis for all their future choices. They will carry this message of this all-encompassing invisible power of the Universe to others who would hear until one day, perhaps, all mankind will be conscious of this great power that heals, provides, enlightens, and builds up all to be happy, joyous and free."

Terry sat back in his seat and took a long deep breath, closed his eyes and smiled. "It's not just about blowing. It even comes out in words! Woo Hoo!" he shouted.

"OK, Sadoval, drop us off here an' you go on to yer old cabin in the Chuskas. We'll take care a' yer job at the mine," said the Old Man and the trio got out at the outskirts of a small village at the intersection of New Mexico Highway 605 and Route 66.

"Does he really know what to do?" asked John as they watched the Desoto disappear down the highway. "I'm not sure I really understand it."

"O it don't matter if'n ya' understand, Johnny, what matters is that you realize," and the Old Man stuck out his thumb as they started walking north on Highway 605.

Realize what, John thought. *Maybe he means the Plan. That must be it, that plan that starts with choosing love over fear. Hmmm.".*

Chapter Seven: John's Second Awakening

It was a cool and cloudless morning in the high desert. You could feel the beginning of the Sun's warmth as it enlivened the bright leathery landscape that bore the ruggedness of eons yet presented its soft beauty so perfectly in the present moment. The trio walked briskly in silence, the Old Man in the lead, Terry a few steps behind and John bringing up the rear. John thought about Sadoval and how old he must be, over one hundred he figured if he placed their time period as being somewhere in the 1950's. Sadoval was anything but a teetering old man, he was quite robust, and his eyes had sparkled with life.

Life, John mused, and a wave of shame over his past descended upon him once more. *Life. What is the point of it?* He had tried hard to be a good person, doing the right thing establishing a family and a career in Social Work and trying to help people. Now it looked like he had thrown it away on alcohol. This despair started to engulf him in spite of feeling the new hope growing inside. And what a mess he made this time. He had really blown it, but this was not the first time. His first marriage when he was a full-time musician was a blur of traveling gigs, drunkenness and one-night trysts. Well they were not one-nighters for him.

Any women he slept with was 'the one', that special person he could spend the rest of his life with, a feeling he had in the moment with 'her' but which he worked hard to dismiss when he got home to his wife.   This exacerbated his cognitive dissonance which only more drinking could numb.

It was a merry-go-round and roller coaster way of life. Actually, the one-nighters didn't occur until later in his first marriage when he would often get so drunk that he blacked out and woke up in the middle of the night in a car with a strange woman, or, worse yet, it was morning in an unknown apartment.   Then he was really in trouble.   How could he explain to his wife where he had been?   Even with a gig ending at one in the morning he should still be home before dawn after tearing down the equipment and packing it into the truck.   He often used the story of falling asleep at the wheel and having to pull over for a while, but that only worked when gigs were out of town.   The lies kept piling up which only escalated his drinking.   Blackouts became more frequent until that fateful day when he stole a car and took off West.   *West*.   That was where he would find what he needed.   A new life, that was it.   He would turn his back on everything he had done and start fresh.   He was no good to her anyway.   He had even left a letter that she was better off without him.   No one would know him in this new life so he could re-write it and become the person he had always wanted to be. A good person, trustworthy, loyal, kind, brave... (John shook his head. He was reciting the cub scout oath, for God's sake! Was that his idea of who he wanted to be? (In point of fact, he was not really sure who that was, or is, or could be!).

He re-wrote his life all right, at first. He quit drinking, married a kind lovely woman, joined a good church, got involved in community charities and made many new friends. He did his best to keep his old life out of his mind, and he covered up his shame and guilt over it by being extremely active and keeping his mind focused on others. He thought he should do something more with his life than just playing music. Besides, he thought, being a musician was kids' stuff and he had to grow up. So, he went back to college, got his master's in psychology and went to work helping people. He focused his attention on the deep psychological problems of his clients and ignored his own. Four years later, even with a new baby, he was drinking again, blacking out and doing god knows what while destroying his family and possibly his entire life. John's shame and guilt was boiling underneath and he drank even more to try to wash it away. But it wouldn't go away, and he could not control his drinking either. Guilt, shame and addiction to alcohol. He was fighting a battle he could not win. Now here he was in this bizarre situation feeling the full brunt of his shame with no way to escape. He was totally immersed in morbid reflection on the wreckage of his past, having completely forgotten about yesterday's marvelous revelations, and he felt like he was going to jump out of his skin.

His feet were sore. He was tired and hungry. He looked at the sky, the sun was about midday height. He could not understand how those other two could be walking so energetically. John was slowing down and dragging his feet.

"Why do we have to walk? Can't you just snap your fingers or something?" John whined. Silence. "I mean nobody's come by since that first pick-up. Hey! What happened to your dune buggy anyway?" Still silence. "I mean, come on! Can't you just materialize some hamburgers or something!?" John stopped and waited. The two kept walking. "What are you robots or something? I can't keep going like this. It's too hard!" He watched them continue up the road. "I'm not going to move until you *do* something! Come on! It's time for a break at least!" John stopped and stared in complete disbelief. "Are you guys deaf! Hey!" John whistled. "I'm over here!" He was more than tired and impatient now. His anger was building. These two guys were really starting to piss him off. "Hey, assholes! I'm talking to *you!*"

Terry and the Old Man stopped but did not turn around or speak. Immediately John felt shame and guilt for what he had just said. He felt scared that they would never talk to him again. He was afraid they would leave him there - that they would abandon him, and he would once again be alone with no place to go and no purpose. They were like judges in long black robes standing with their backs to him as if declaring he was shunned, worthless, lower than worm slime and condemned to a fate worse than death, whatever that might be. He was so ashamed he collapsed to his knees with his head down and tears welled up. It seemed his whole life was rolled up into these three words: shame, guilt and abandonment. He had been shamed, shamed others and felt ashamed since he could remember. He felt guilty about almost everything he did so he inevitably acted out that guilt and did increasingly worse things. Most of all he felt alone, lonely and abandoned thus leaving a trail of abandonment wherever he went and with everyone he had known. And now he had probably just alienated the only two friends he had left.

John wept.

"Ain't too pretty a picture is it Johnny," the Old Man was standing over John. He put his hand on John's shoulder and squeezed it tightly, so tightly John could feel a pressure go down his arm and through his entire body. The pressure went

up to his head and built and built until he almost screamed in panic that his head would explode and leave a its shrapnel strewn all over the road. Just when he thought he could not stand it any longer his thoughts seemed to burst into a thousand fragments. It felt like the top of his head opened up and poured out thought upon thought like confetti into the sky. It was that column of energy again flowing out of his head but instead of it going and coming from the sky like before, it expanded out all around him forming a glowing aura of energy encircling his body and growing. It was not coming from the Old Man or the sky, it was coming from somewhere deep inside him, as if it had been buried there all along under those layers of guilt, anger and fear, all of which had just been released from him and dissolved in mid-air.

John felt light.

"He's a-glowin' ain't he Terry," said the Old Man.

"He shore is!" Terry replied in a delightfully satisfied voice.

"I'm, I'm sorry guys. Sorry I yelled at you," sobbed John.

"You jes' forgot who you was again, Johnny. It happens to all of us once in a while. Gradually it goes away, though," said the Old Man.

Terry looked into John's eyes with a love so great that John's fears melted away into nothingness. "And I didn't even have to wave my hand. You did that all on your own."

"But the Old Man, he put his hand on me and I felt something," said John his sobs now subsiding.

"Aww, I was jus' tryin' to add a little drama,' said the Old Man. "Whole thing was yer own doin'. You got it in you to correct yerself now when ya' go off halfcocked like ya jes' did. I came over to help remind you of that."

"You see, John," explained Terry, "when a person is ready, they are ready. But we sometimes need another's helping hand to remind us. You just peeled off another layer of what's been eating you all your life. Your Dad was never there for you. He was always out drinking, gambling and carousing leaving you feeling lonely and abandoned. Your Mom was an emotional basket case who screamed, yelled and slapped you into a pile of shame and guilt leaving you bitter, angry and resentful. But you always had something going for you, an invisible something that carried you through even the worst of times. It was as simple as an elusive figure hiding in the basement, or some kind of force or power getting you out of jams like the time you were lost in the swamp. Or, as seemingly complex as an Old Man in a dune buggy saving you from the desert. But it always came from you, out of you, from deep inside. You have always carried your own salvation with you and now it's all out in the open and you are really free!"

"How do you know all this?" John hesitated.

A voice came out of Terry that filled the desert. "To some it comes all at once like it did to me. To others it comes in stages. Either way is as good as the other. The point is we have found the basis of life to be love, peace and harmony and we move forward impelled by this, not fear.

John felt the pressure go completely off his shoulders and body. He felt even lighter than before, like this time he really would fly. John jumped to his feet and shouted in a singing voice, "I'm free! I'm free!" The Old Man held out another guitar and waved it in front of John. Ignoring how ludicrous it was for the Old Man to be standing in the middle of the desert materializing a guitar, he grabbed it and transformed this new joy into a new song:

I'm free as a bird, joy in perfect flight,
Love in all places, everything is light.
Free to enjoy, to live, love and learn,
The world is my kingdom and everything is clear...
Everything is clear!

The chorus rang through the desert as if it were echoing across a huge canyon. More words came as an invisible orchestra and choir played and sang with him:

Stop and listen! What do you hear?
Voices of angels, in the air.
Heard in the wind, heard in the trees,
Heard in your mind saying you are free!

Free as a bird, joy in perfect flight,
Love in all places, everything is light.
Free to enjoy, to live, love and learn,
The world is your kingdom and everything is clear...
Everything is clear!

I am loving, I give my hand to you,
I am here, all you need to do,
Just relax and put your mind at ease,
There is no other power let go and release.

Trust in your mind: the thoughts I give to you,
You can believe, have faith that it's all true.
There is no other power, let go and release.
Know the perfect love. Everything is peace...
Everything is peace.

Choose to listen to the voice of God,
Quietly within you, a whisper and a nod.
Speaking your nature. Speaking the truth:
There's nothing left but love and giving love to you!

Free as a bird, joy in perfect flight,
Love in all places, everything is light.

Free to enjoy, to live, love and learn,
The world is your kingdom and everything is clear...
Everything is clear...everything is clear... everything is clear...
Everything is clear!

"And so it is!" Terry declared.

John finished the last strum of the guitar and drank in the stillness. Peace flowed from him and Terry and permeated the landscape. Everything was silent, the silence of eternal peace. And the Old Man was gone.

Chapter Eight: John and Terry Regroup

John could now clearly see Terry's gifts: his ability to calm down a volatile situation and his incredible insight into new situations no matter how unique or startling. He had seen what the Old Man could do, at least he thought it was the Old Man doing it, like time travel and knowing things in ways beyond John's comprehension. But now he wondered what his gifts were. What was he supposed to do? He felt he had nothing to offer, no magic in his hand or time travel abilities. And just when he had really begun to trust the Old Man to guide him, he disappears. Now there was no Old Man to tell him what to do next, so he looked to Terry.

"Terry, what're we supposed to do now? Are we still stuck back in the fifties? Can you time travel? Didn't the Old Man tell Sadoval we were going to the mine and take care of his job? Do you know where the mine is? What should we tell them if we find it? Is the Old Man coming back for us? Where did he go anyway? What is going to- "

"Ho-old o-on tha-ar!" said Terry with the same emphasis he had always put on that phrase when they were kids. "I don't know where the Old Man is, and I have no answers to any of those questions."

"Well then who does?"

"Well, that, my dear friend you will have to ask yourself."

"Aw come on, Terry! Quit it! We could really be in trouble, here in the middle of nowhere, or, uh, no *when!*"

"Look, remember when the Old Man asked me to tell Sadoval what was going on?'

"Yeah, in the car early this morning."

"I didn't know what to say. There was nothing going through my mind. *Nothing.* But I trusted myself to guide me and I opened my mouth and as I spoke, words came out. You heard them. And they made sense"

"Yeah, I wondered how you knew all that stuff, Mr. Brainy."

"I didn't know. That's the point. Like what about when we first met Sadoval and you started running down the mountainside toward the cavalry, did you know what to do before you started?"

"Hey, I was pushed."

"Yeah and it gave you no time to think. You just acted. If you had thought about it you probably would have tried to get into a discussion with the Old Man. Then you never would have acted. As it turns out, you did a great job."

"Uh, yeah, he went that-a-way! He went that-a-way!"

"Well it worked, didn't it?"

"So you gonna push me, Terry, to wake me up?"

"Naw. Well...maybe. You just need to slow down and stop thinking for a minute. Look at those beautiful rock formations over there. Isn't this amazing country? I always loved the southwest, the deserts, the mountains. Hey, Monument Valley and the Petrified Forest! How about Canyon De Chelly! Great stuff. We should we go there!"

John stopped thinking about their situation and pondered the scenery. He drank in the majestic beauty of the distant mountains and the nearby mesas. He thought about all the places he had never gotten around to visiting. In his mind's eye he saw the Painted Desert, the Black Mesa, the Little Colorado River Gorge and the Grand Canyon. He opened his arms and drew all these wonders into his consciousness and saw himself skipping and dancing among them.

John snapped out of it with an idea.

"Terry! The mining! You know something about it, right? And the Old Man sure seemed focused on it. Sadoval is off chanting and 'Medicine Waying' to help his people for that very thing, all that cancer and sickness caused by radiation and radon gas and stuff. There was a reason we went back and saved that young prospector, but the reason doesn't make sense. Why would we save a guy just in time for him to direct another guy toward what turned out to be the biggest uranium find in the country, that caused so many deaths and such misery for the Navajos? Shouldn't we have tried to change things?"

"I know this much, John. This is not about changing the past. You can't change the past, except where the past is not yet past. But I can't get into that right now. The point is, you needed to see some things and so did I but on a universal timeless plane, not on the worldly plane of existence."

"So this isn't about keeping a disaster from happening that already happened?"

"Oh, no, not at all. Think about it from these new revelations we've had. This is about changing hearts not events. Look at history. It's full of disasters caused by greed, ignorance and lust for power. There have been genocides worse than the Navajos and some not so bad. Sometimes reparations were made. But man always fell into another bad situation fueled by his own weaknesses and fears. No sooner was one problem dealt with when a new one came up. Problem, solution; problem, solution. And are we any happier than we were, say, 2000 years ago? No, the solution is not to try and fix these problems, the solution is to find an entirely different basis upon which to make our choices. What we have discovered. Our new revelation! That peace, love and harmony are it! They are the real thing! Now we can live beyond them and watch problems dissolve away around us with seemingly no effort on our part. We just show up and let the motives for our actions take the lead. I love it! Peace love and harmony. Wow! What incredible motives!"

"Oh, yeah, I see. New problems will always come up and we need a power greater than anything mankind can devise to...to...not to solve them...but...but...to make completely different choices! Choices that work! Choices based on love, peace, joy and harmony!" John was a whirlwind of revelations.

"Yeah, the choice is left to you."

"OH MY GOD! My song! *Choose your pain and misery or choose the higher ride.* How can we get all those people to make different choices? And how do we know what choice they should make?"

"We don't John and that's none of our business. Our business to be right with ourselves, to make our choice to let go of all our own pain and misery. There's no one to do that for us. No god or savior that will take our suffering from us if only we ask, because it's already been given. So that leaves it entirely up to us. We must let it all go. And when we let go, miracles seem to happen like helping Sadoval and that prospector. Like us meeting. But that is only the beginning. Why don't you choose to let go and see what happens next? You'll never know until you give it a try."

"Yeah, right, Terry. We're out in the desert, remember. So I'm just supposed to sit here and let go of all the stuff from my entire past and then we're saved?"

"What do you think?"

" Aren't you worried, Terry?"

"About what?"

"About anything?"

"No."

"No regrets? No anger? No shame, guilt, fear?"

"No."

"Not pissed at your Dad anymore? Don't want to get high? Nothing?"

"Nope."

"You let it all go?"

"Yup."

"Just like that?" John snapped his fingers.

"Seems so."

"Okay, you got it all together. You choose. Choose what we do next."

"You're not getting off that easy, John."

"Why shouldn't it be you. You're the one who has none of the baggage from the past. It's all gone for you. No anger, resentment, et cetera, *et cetera.* So you choose. What you choose would be good, right?"

"As clever as you think you are being, John, you're only fooling yourself. It is you that must make the decision for you and only for you. Let go. Then you will know."

"Know what?"

"Oh, here we go again. Just shut up and do it!"

"Hey, hey, I thought we were friends, Terry ma boy?"

"Do it NOW!!!"

"Okay, okay, okay! I GIVE UP!"

What happened next seemed at first to be nothing at all. John and Terry were still standing alongside the road. It was still mid-day, and nothing had changed. Quietly, like a tiny voice had told him to, John simply looked down at his feet and started walking. He had no thoughts of where he was going or what was going to happen. He just watched with fascination as he put one foot in front of the other. He looked at each spot as his foot touched it, one spot after another. With each step he felt more confident. Entranced with this step by step movement, he did not look ahead. He did not look behind. He watched as he walked with absolutely no concern about where he was going or when he would get there. That tiny new voice in his head knew the key was in the journey right here and now, not in the destination. And John was listening, finally listening. Words to a song an old friend had written came to him.

Step by step, inch by inch, hour by hour and day by day,
We travel the road and ease our load,
Step by step. Step by Step.

Step by Step, we receive the power.
Step by step, we're happy, joyous and free!
Step by step, we return to Spirit.
Step by step, we find eternity.

The words played over and over in his mind. He thought of nothing else. He saw only his feet moving. Time and space temporarily disappeared, and he literally felt as one with all of life in a timeless peace.

Two boys with stick guns were about to face the largest most powerful enemy in the world, say 'Bang! Bang!' and win the battle for both sides.

(End of Second Movement)

Second Interlude:

The Uranium King

"So now you're telling me how to run my company!?" William Maestro paced back and forth in front of the glass wall that separated him from the sprawling metropolis below.

"No, no, Bill! It's these reports from the EPA! They're conclusive and about to go public! We've got to do something!"

Maestro took a deep calming breath and perused the man shouting at him from across his desk. Dan Kroeger, his loyal friend, prospecting partner and now right-hand man at International Petroleum Corporation. He sat down hard in his cushy leather chair.

"I know you're not the enemy, Dan, but we've been keeping this under wraps for twenty years. Exposure now could put a halt to production. What with demands for Uranium decreasing the way it is, this could put our Canadian and Australian competitors back on top, to say nothing of Africa!"

"There are always solutions. We can call an emergency board meeting- "

"Forget it, Dan. Most of the board has remained voluntarily blind to the hazards in the mines. We've got to figure a way through this before we present anything." Maestro remembered the first time EPA reports could not be ignored. That was in Colorado when high levels of radon gas were detected in a handful of private homes. They had successfully orchestrated a 'full cleanup' of all affected communities and had satisfied the government and the public that all hazards were removed and there was no longer anyone at risk. But that was not on Navajo Land, and the risk to the Navajos had never been addressed. The token clean-up and positive press releases calmed everything down for a few years, but now - He and Dan were the only ones who knew the whole story on the Navajo mines coverup. To date, the Navajo Nation and the U.S. government remained officially ignorant of the detrimental effects of exposure in the mines and, with so many of the original mines already closed, and the tailings and run off that had begun to contaminate their lands... Maestro didn't even know to what extent the Indians were affected. But it seems the EPA now had an inkling. In the midst of this cacophony of thoughts, a tiny voice inside his head whispered, *What about the people!*

Dan shook the papers in his hand. "I think the biggest problem is their reference to the original treaty, *all lands will be restored to their original condition.* We both know the mines were closed but never sealed up and with only minimal cleanup and no land restoration. And now they have all these reports of contamination in the waters, the livestock, the very mortar they use in the walls and floors of their homes! Mortar made from the sandy runoff from the mines themselves!"

Maestro tried to take another deep breath, but his breathing had become shallow and his heart was racing. *What about the people!* the voice whispered again. This had always been about success. His thoughts turned to his prospecting days with Dan in the Chuskas over twenty years ago, how he had beamed with arrogant confidence that they would surely succeed on their great adventure. And succeed they did! Greater than their expectations. Then there were their subsequent discoveries of petroleum deposits in Canada, Australia and South America. They were in great demand by the big companies because of their skill at finding rich deposits of ore and petroleum. Eventually, he was able to fulfill his childhood dream of sitting in the big chair of his own company. And it had all worked! Except that he had no idea the discovery of radium, plutonium and the A-bomb would also create much more than wealth and success. He felt like he was trapped on that cliff again, but this time, no one to bail him out. *What about the people!* Could he admit to himself that their ventures were destroying families and endangering an entire people? In his heart, he had never intended to ignore the rights and safety of anyone. He had gotten caught in the whirlwind of success. Now guilt had boiled to the surface. He had obligations to his board, investors, partners, an entire network of companies that depended on these uranium mine profits. But, *what about the People...?*

"Look, Bill, we've got to weigh the pros and cons of the situation. What we can do to minimize the damage. How many resources and funds we can direct to satisfying the EPA demands. Clean-up of some sort is inevitable, but we'll have to minimize the costs and maximize the results-"

"That's Enough! Enough of this!" Maestro stood up. "I know the deal! It's the same old same old! Here we go again. Another roller coaster ride into the depths so we can eventually come out on top! Pros and cons. Pros and cons. How can we save our asses this time!" He turned to the wall of window and looked hopelessly out at the city. The skyscrapers were like giant wailing walls filled with mourners. "More fires to put out. Always fires. So many fires." *What about the people.*

Kroeger said nothing. Maestro waved his arm behind his back and said, "Go Dan. Just go. I need time to think."

He heard the door close and continued staring out the window. People. The world is made of people. People with homes and families. Had he forgotten that in his quest for success? No. No. No! Wasn't he a decent sort of fellow? Had he not treated people fairly? Oh, but how many times did he turn a blind eye. Yes, there were deals, white lies, threats, stepping on toes. But now he was beginning to realize just what effect his dealings were having on the fate of the Navajo People.

The intercom buzzed him out of his morass. "Mr. Maestro, there are two men in the outside lobby to see you." *Oh shit, were they here already!?* "They say they are from a government agency, the Battle Brigade?"

The Battle Brigade, he thought. *What kind of-* "Aw, Hell! Send them in!"

Maestro sat at his desk and pretended to organize some papers as the two men walked in. Both were neatly dressed in modest blue serge suits with white shirts and striped neckties. The one on the left was tall and gaunt, yet his checks were rosy and his eyes gleamed. The shorter stocky one was smiling from ear to ear, which Maestro didn't like so much.

"Why, William. William Maestro. It's me, John. The guy that saved you from that cliff. Remember? Me and the Old Man in the dune buggy?" Maestro looked closely at John's face, gasped, and stiffened like he had just been hit with a taser.

"Aw, come on, Billy Boy. He saved you once. Don't think he won't do it again," said Terry.

"Y-you look so young," stammered Maestro.

"You know Terry here was saying that same thing just the other day. Must be my healthy eating." John pointed at Terry. "This is Terry, Terry Silverman."

Maestro exhaled loudly. "What is-? "

"What is. What is." Terry interjected. "He's already askin' the right question, eh Johnny?"

"He sho-o-ore is!" John quickly interjected in Terry's own vernacular. "A good question *is* its own answer."

"*What* certainly *is,* and 'what is' *is* what is, 'cause what isn't can't exist with 'what is' around. And 'what is' certainly is all around us, now, isn't it?" posed Terry.

Maestro buried his head in his hands. 'OOOH, I must be dreaming. I must be dreaming. When did I fall asleep?" He looked up again and the two men were still there, looking at him inquiringly as if they were waiting for him to do something.

"So, Mister Maestro," John said lyrically, "exactly why have you called this meeting?"

"Meeting? I called? What are you talking about?"

"Yes, indeedy, this meeting of your minds. Good mind. Bad mind. Out of your mind. Seems something must be on your mind. Something disturbing, perhaps? Something gnawing on your conscience maybe? You got a mind full. Come on, Bill, spill," John seriously quipped.

These two men had discombobulated Maestro so completely, he was unable to shore himself up into business mode. He slapped his hands against his cheeks and pushed hard trying to compress his thoughts into something intelligible. His heart raced. Face flushed, he felt drops of perspiration on his forehead. Pressing his lips tightly together, blowing his cheeks up like balloons, he blurted out, "WHAT ABOUT THE PEOPLE!?" and slumped back in his chair.

"The people," Terry began to narrate, "or 'dine' as they call themselves, refers to the Navajo nation, an indigenous American people now living on a reservation that spans Utah, Arizona and New Mexico mainly south of the Four Corners. A race of people mostly peaceful, by nature, who have no word for revenge as they view bad, evil or sinful behavior as a sickness rather than a free will moral choice. Their ways include many healing ceremonies meant to cure their enemies of their sickness rather than destroy them, although they have been known to attack enemies from time to time when backed into a corner with their families and lands threatened."

"You know, *people,* includes you, too, Bill. Don't leave yourself out," said John empathetically.

Terry and John sat in their chairs across the desk from Maestro as he stared at them eyes filling with tears. The dam burst and the pain and guilt he had suppressed for two decades spewed forth. With each heavy sob of emotional pain came a sense of relief, a lightening of the burden he had been shouldering for so long. He became oblivious of the two men, the room, his logical thoughts. Everything else was supplanted by this emotional pain/relief he was experiencing. He could feel his heart changing, yet, not changing, but being realized in its true form. A feeling of love welled up from inside, of peace, harmony, something no words could fully describe. Nothing had changed except in his own head. *Not even my head,* he thought. It was like it came from somewhere deeper inside him than anyone could physically go. Deeper than mind, deeper than body, yet inside his own self, not from anywhere else. And something *had* changed. He felt light, lighter than air, as if he had always been able to float, but a great weight had been pressing down, holding him from taking off into the air. Now the heaviness was gone. The pressure, gone. And he was floating! Floating, and full of such a joy that- they all began laughing simultaneously.

"Ha, ha, ha, ha, hoo, hoo, ha, ha, hee, hee, hee, ho, ho, ha, ha! Ha-ah, hah, hah, hah, whoo, hoo, ho, hoo, hee, hee, hee, hee, whoo, whoo, hah, hah! Wha-a-a-a-h, hah, hah, hah, hah, hah, hah, hah, ho, ho, ho, ho, hee, hee, hee! Whe-e-ee, hee, hee, hee, hee, hee, hee, hee, hah, hah, hah, hah, ho, ho, who! Wha-a-a-ah, ha, ha, ha, ha, ha, ha, ha, hah, hah, ho, ho, hee, he, who!"

John stood up and grabbed Terry's hand, Terry reached out to a very different William Maestro who, without thinking, came around the desk and grabbed his hand. They followed John in a circle and began dancing. Around and around they danced. Faster and faster. Laughing and dancing. William was so excited and happy, he hardly took notice when a large campfire appeared in the center of their circle, or when the drums began beating, or when the shrill chant of a thousand singers pierced the air, or when he saw the sparks of the campfire rising into the star-studded black canopy above. They were joined by many men and women from Buckskin Dancers to African Dancers. Each dancer was clothed differently in an indescribably colorful costume. These new dancers waved their hands like they were throwing things into the fire, so William pretended he was throwing things into the fire. With each toss, he felt even lighter. He pictured pieces of paper with words in his own handwriting being burned. Words like, *shame, guilt, exploitation, greed, power, lust, fear, hate, monster, evil, destruction* and *death.* Then he pictured other words like *good, mind, body, health, happiness, healing, fix, desire, want, search* and *improve* burning in the fire. The fire was taking away every part of his self, and his feelings were a mixture of burning grief and ecstatic joy. Out of the ashes he was beginning to sense a new person growing from the depths of the glowing flames and ready to burst out. He could feel love, peace and harmony growing out from the center of his heart. The chanting rose to a height that consumed all his senses. It was a language he had never heard before, but the words seemed to translate clearly in his brain.

Fire, fire, cleanse my heart of all desire;
Fire, fire, turn the darkness now to light;
Leave me empty, leave me pure, so I can be a living cure.
As the ashes disappear, I see only love so pure.

They continued for what seemed like hours to William, who was so filled with joy he wanted it never to end. With that thought, he realized it would never end, because it never began. It always is. He simply had never seen it until now. *What is,* he thought as he danced. *What is, what is, what is, what is! What is is all there is and all there is is beautiful!*

This is how William joined the ranks of those who realize peace, harmony and love as the essence of all things. He could now see, feel, live and breathe infinite joy. From that day forth, he no longer based his decision-making on weighing the pros and cons, debits and credits, good and bad. He no longer obsessed about himself and his own fate. He no longer saw people as instruments to his own ends. He no longer saw the world filled with problems that had to be fixed. Instead, he continued through the rest of his life being a joy and a blessing to everyone around him, and everything he did was of benefit to all parties, no just to himself and his interests. He took joy in watching those who would, wake up and see. He was delighted to give forth everything he had in every given moment because he knew he was drawing from an infinite source of supply and love, an infinite source that lived within his own being.

As the sun peaked between the tops of the Chuska Mountains to the east, sending beams of light across the high desert, John, Terry and William unclasped their hands, and William sat back in his cushy chair behind his desk smiling to a quiet empty room.

And this is how John and Terry began to continue the battle they had begun as little boys, now armed with the three most powerful weapons in the world: love, peace and harmony.

Third Movement:
The Path of Home

Chapter One: The Uranium Mine

"I think we're here," Terry's voice said from behind him. John had been marching up the deserted desert road to the beat of the words of his old friend's song, *Step By Step,* feeling unburdened, alive and free floating in a timeless joy.

He now looked up to see a guardhouse and a high security gate right in front of him. Above the gate was a sign that read 'Crystal Mines: International Petroleum Corporation'. It seemed like only moments ago they were alone in the desert with no civilization for miles. And the sun indicated it was still midday, yet John was not perplexed by any of this.

He turned to Terry very calmly and said, "You'd better speak to the guard now." He almost added, 'Terry boy'.

Terry stepped up to the open window of the guardhouse and politely said, "Excuse me, sir."

A man in a dark green uniform, his head buried in a newspaper, jerked his head up with a start. "Hey where'd you come from?"

"We're friends of Sadoval Whitehorse, the old Navajo that works here?" Terry continued.

"Whitehorse? Hmmm...Whitehorse. let me think." The guard no longer appeared concerned about their sudden appearance. "Um, yeah, that crazy old Indian who serves lunch. Now, what about him?"

"Mr. Whitehorse will not be back to work," replied Terry.

"Yup, he's gone off to pray for his people." John chimed in cheerfully.

"Pray for his people? What the hell! Damn Navajos, always takin' off like that! Whose gonna get lunch for all those miners?"

Terry and John looked at each other and smiled. "We'll do it, sir," they said in unison.

"Nah, nah, ya got no clearance," the guard said impatiently. He squared up his shoulders, scrutinized them suspiciously and said quite empathically, "Say, who *are* you boys anyway?"

John expected Terry to do the hand-gesture blowing thing but instead he said, "Well, we run the Gallup Employment Agency and, instead of sending out a new man, well, we couldn't find one so quickly anyway, we thought we'd come ourselves to help out. Just for today, I mean."

"Yeah, just for today," John added.

"Yeah. We'll get a new man out here tomorrow but it's lunchtime already and we have little time to prepare," Terry said assuredly

"But, I don't think-"

"Oops, there's the whistle, I think. Terry didn't you hear the noon whistle?"

"Yup. That's the noon whistle alright. We'd better get going," Terry said hurriedly.

"But I don't hear-"

"Well if ain't, it's gonna be any second," John said. "Look at the clock! Come on now! Open the gate! We got work to do!"

The guard mechanically reached down and pushed the 'gate' button as he gazed blankly at the two strangers.

"Thanks, sir! We'll be back after lunch!" Terry called over his shoulder as they both rushed through the gate.

"Yeah, and we'll put a good word in for ya'. The boys are sure gonna be happy they didn't miss out on mealtime. You're a good man," John added, and he looked down at his feet, took a step, and they were in the cafeteria.

The whistle blew just as they rushed into the kitchen. It smelled of Mexican food and, naturally, all the ovens were hot and loaded with fully cooked food ready to be eaten so they put on aprons and oven mitts and started lining up the pans of hot food on the serving counter. As the men, all Navajo, began piling in, Terry and John were ready with serving spoons: enchiladas, refried beans, rice, corn tortillas, lettuce and pico de gallo. John was neither curious nor startled. He felt confident as he sprang into action and served the men. His acceptance of new and strange circumstances had developed for him and he loved it. It was like magic. Everything needed was provided with no effort on his part. All he had to do was show up and go to work. He felt he could do anything, and that the possibilities were limitless, but standing there now serving lunch was exactly where he belonged and felt like the most wonderful thing he could be doing at the moment.

Mostly, the miners were speaking Navajo, but John had no trouble understanding the language of hunger. Each man received a heaping plate of food down to the last miner. There seemed to be no bottom to the pans as the two addicts turned enlightened turned servants kept scooping out the food. After everyone was served each pan was still at least half full. Terry and John leaned their elbows on the counter, chins in their hands and gazed at the crowd.

"I bet the men haven't seen this good a lunch ever out here," Terry said.

"I didn't even know enchiladas were invented in the nineteen fifties," mused John.

"Most of these mines don't have cafeterias. I used to study Navajo history at the library whenever I went into Shiprock for supplies back when I lived in the trailer over in Arizona. This must be the big mine that makes all the money."

"Hmmm, must be, or shall I say, *must have been,* lots of money in uranium." John said with an air of knowledge as he was now totally used to not worrying about their mysterious jaunts through time.

"It made a lot of big businesses rich and provided plutonium for a lot of atom bombs. In fact, after World War II, the demand was so great, fueled mostly by the Bureau of Atomic Energy and of course the quest for profits by big oil companies and mining subsidiaries, that the dangers of radiation exposure were downplayed, even ignored. It wasn't just ignorance, it was deceit. The Navajos agreed to the mining companies coming in as long as they could work the mines and get some of the profits. They weren't told about the hazards and, for a while, became clueless guinea pigs for the government. Without the Navajos' knowledgeable consent, the BAE used them to monitor the effects of radiation exposure over time. They even had medical teams caravanning all over the Rez taking blood and urine samples, x-rays and all that without ever telling the people anything about it. Even after the dangers of radiation were exposed, it was only the non-Indians, off reservation land like to the north in Colorado, that were warned, and measures taken to rid homes of radon gas exposure. It turned out even the walls and floors of homes built in the sixties and seventies on the Rez were made of radioactive adobe brick from sand they gathered from tailings that washed down from the mines. I used to wish that I could have gone back in time and warned everyone. Thousands of lives could have been saved.

But now I understand the bigger picture, the one you and I have stepped into, been called to. The one we are sharing now and will continue to share wherever we go. Mankind has never been able to stop the greed and lust for power and all its devastating consequences. The two of us maybe can't. But we can live and be in this new way, this way of surrendering, letting go, loving. This way of forgiveness. This way of peace. We can be it, share it and watch it grow. And we can find others who are ready and willing."

"Hey, just like the Old Man did with us!"

"Yes, and, just like him, we have work to do. Look around the room, John. Do you see that kind of glowing over the men?"

"It's like all those men put together are giving off a shimmer that kind of radiates just above their heads."

"Yeah, and that's not radioactivity. But, look over there. That one man has it going higher than the rest, like a spike on an oscilloscope."

"That's the man to talk to, ya think?"

"I do believe you are right, John. Hold on, he's getting up. I think he's coming for seconds."

"You two men, do I know you from somewhere?" The dark-skinned man had a long single braid down his back and looked Navajo or Mexican to John, but he spoke very good English with hardly a trace of an accent.

"Yeah, howdy, how's it goin'?" queried John trying to sound like he fit in.

"How is *what* going?" said the Navajo with a confused look.

John whispered over to Terry, "Oh, yeah, 1950's."

"Right," said Terry fastidiously.

"Name's John. This here's Terry. How are you doing?"

"How am I doing what?" the man looked even more bewildered.

John felt like he was visiting another planet. "Hmm, thought that one would work," John glanced sideways at Terry.

"Oh, we're from the catering service. You like the Mexican style lunch we brought?" asked Terry.

"Yes. Sure. That's why I came up. This isn't the usual fare Sadoval Whitehorse serves. It is really quite good, but...uh, different."

"Quite, quite...hmmm...yes, we, uh, just invented it. I think we'll call it Tex-Mex, that sound good to you, John?" John nodded assuredly and added, "Oh, you'll be seeing a lot more of this kind of food in the next couple a' decades."

"Risky business laying something new like this on these miners," the man pointed out. "They are very traditional and set in the Navajo ways. I am surprised there is no grumbling about, but everyone seems quite happy with lunch today."

"Yes, quite," said Terry and John in tandem still resting their chins on their hands, elbows on the counter.

"Oh, by the way, my name is Hector, Hector Perez. I am not so traditional. Sent off to boarding school back in the 1930's and got a very good education, a white education, if you know what I mean."

"So it seems," said Terry and John added, "So how do you happen to be working the mines?"

"Well I ended up with a degree in Geology and went off to teach High School in Santa Fe. Then, just after World War II, I heard about the big push to find uranium. Being the inquisitive sort, I wrote a letter to the Mining Commission up in Colorado asking if there were any opportunities for a degreed geologist. They directed me to the Bureau of Atomic Energy and before I knew it, I was prospecting for uranium instead of teaching school. I found the mother lode here. When the government confirmed I was one-hundred percent Navajo, they said I could stake the claim, but one of the white-owned companies would have to mine it. So, here I am a partner with International Petroleum helping dig my fortune..." He gazed into the distance. "Funny thing is, I really don't care about getting rich. Haven't seen much money from it either. Makes me wonder what I'm really doing here."

"Now that's just the kinda question me and Johnny can help you find the answer to," Terry said in a whimsical yet serious tone.

Hector looked at Terry and John suspiciously. Terry blew across his palm toward Hector and all three started walking toward the doorway with John at the lead. They stepped out of the cafeteria and beheld the front entrance to Santa Fe High School. Hector stood motionless, his lunch plate in a death grip, and gasped. Terry put his hand on Hector's shoulder and John spoke quite articulately.

"This is where you belong, Hector. You have finished your role in the mines. The students here at the high school are your legacy. As a science teacher, you need to be teaching them science. As an individual, you need to practice a new consciousness that goes far beyond everyday living."
Terry interrupted John's reverie before it turned into one of his long speeches. "Whaddaya say we go up to the science lab?" he suggested.

Hector took the lead hesitantly then more quickly as, with each step, his excitement grew. "I haven't been here in over three years. It's like coming home!" His enthusiasm seemed to have overcome his bewilderment at being there, over one hundred miles from the mine, in only a few seconds.

Hector practically ran into the science lab, the two friends right behind him. He stood behind his old desk and ran one palm across its smooth rubbery gray surface. "Ahhh. My old desk!" He looked over the empty lab at all the student

tables, each with test tubes, Bunsen burners and various tools set neatly on clean towels ready for the next day's class. There were dozens of rock samples lining the window sills to his right. "We did a lot of rock hunting to get those," he pointed out to the two friends. "The kids always loved the field trips, discovering our land with new vision as I taught them about the composition of the various rock formations. I loved to see the looks in their eyes with every new 'a ha!' as they realized so many new things. You know, that was the most rewarding thing about teaching, not what they learned, but the very experience of learning itself, expanding their minds and seeing the world from a whole new perspective." Hector, still firmly holding his plate, plopped down in his old desk chair and sighed.

"That's the key, isn't it, Hector. A new perspective," said John.

"Yeah, a paradigm shift," added Terry. "We're born one way and practically programmed to believe and act ways that are acceptable in our culture, and we tend not to question them until someone comes along with a fresh perspective and shows us something different."

Hector mused as if talking to the air, "These kids, they all have so much potential, but many of them seem to never reach it, or even worse, take on destructive ways,"

"You know, Hector, you have something these kids really need. And I don't mean just knowledge of geology," said John gently yet firmly. As Hector sat, John could see his facial tension relax and his body sit upright and confident. John opened his mouth and a voice came out that seemed to belong to someone else.

"Your perspective, Hector, is devoid of greed and desire for power and money. You have been side-tracked from your true mission, but your heart has never left this classroom. It is time for you to reaffirm your practice of living according to your true perspective and sharing it by example through your love of teaching and your students. In a fear-ridden world, with disasters looming around every corner, the children need to have an example of love, peace and harmony in their midst. You do not need to teach or preach this perspective. You are it. You live it. All you are required to do is show up and love, peace and harmony will flow out from you like ripples from a pebble dropped in a glassy pool of water. You do not have to expound upon what is wrong in this world or what needs to be righted. Silently and solidly, moment by moment, through your own realizations, you are the embodiment of what the children need." John paused as the three reflected in silence.

"By your example, your students shall have ample opportunity to discover many new things for themselves, within themselves. By your example, your students will be given the opportunity to find their true self inherent in their own being."

Hector was listening intently to John's speech. "These words are not new to me. I have longed to live that way for as long as I can remember. But how...I mean, where...?

"You are already living it. We have just moved instantaneously through time and space. This is not a trick, it is merely a change in perspective, one that science has recently begun to discover. Because you are a scientist, you realize there are still countless unknowns yet to be discovered. Many of your students shall be encouraged through you to find new perspectives, meet new challenges, discover new worlds and much more that is not usually taught in the schools. You will only teach science, for this consciousness for love, peace and harmony are imparted, not taught. You *live* it! *That* is how you impart it!" John stepped back as a conclusion to his speech.

"And don't forget, what you give out to your students will come back to you exponentially," Terry added. "As the poet Robert Browning wrote, 'Open out a way and let the imprisoned splendor escape.' As it does, the problems of the world will decrease as more high school graduates enter the adult world making decisions based on harmony, peace and love."

Terry motioned Hector towards the classroom door, and John followed as the awestruck Hector stepped, not into the school hallway, but back into the cafeteria. They walked over to the serving counter. Hector was still holding his plate in front of him, so Terry plopped an enchilada on it. "Hey, Johnny, he sure has a big glow on him now, don't he?" John thought Terry was sounding more like the Old Man every minute.

Hector gasped. "How did you do that?"

John spoke again. "That doesn't matter right now. What's important is you know in your heart you must go back to teaching science. Leave the mines. Leave the profits. Let them go to your clan, to education, to wherever you feel they could be beneficial. Now you know your purpose and what you must do. So go. Go now. Do it! Make your arrangements!"

"Yeah. It's time to get out of Dodge!" Terry interjected.

Hector took a deep breath and his body relaxed a bit. Instead of speaking, he gave an understanding nod and, still appearing a bit stunned, walked his plate back to the table where he resumed eating in silence, occasionally glancing over at Terry and John.

John knew Hector was ready. He knew because he now trusted that every step he took would provide the persons who were ready and willing to take the next step. He had complete confidence that the words and actions needed would come forth in each moment. And in each moment, he could trust this new consciousness to guide and direct him in ways beneficial to everyone he would encounter.

The whistle blew and the men went back to work. "Well, I suppose we better hang around and clean up the joint 'n all," said John.

"Yep, it's always good to clean up after a good day's work."

Terry rolled a bus cart over to the tables and began clearing and wiping. John started dumping food pans, rinsing them out and placing them in the high-powered commercial dishwashers. There were two dishwashers, four stainless steel sinks and several large food preparation areas in a very large kitchen. This was a much fancier set-up than John expected out in the high desert in the 1950's, but he knew uranium mining was big business and this was, after all, the richest mine on Navajo land. Funny thing though, he did not remember hearing of the Navajos getting rich and living in fancy houses at any time during his lifetime. He felt a pang of guilt for what his people did to their people. Then he remembered that his job was to share his new way of living everywhere he went from this day forward. He realized a remorseful rumbling about what should have been would not help anything. Pointing fingers at business, government or people would only exacerbate dissension and ill will. He was now certain love was the only answer to every question. In this way, his mind and heart were open to the next encounter.

Terry rattled the last cartful of dirty dishes into the kitchen and John rinsed and placed them in the dishwashers.

"Well, looks mighty clean. What say you and I go check on Sadoval," Terry said matter-of-factly as if it were in the plans all along.

"So, you want to walk, take a dune buggy or shall I step right there?"

"I never did get to ride in that buggy. Let me drive, Johnny."

"Hey, I never got to drive it myself? You think you're the Old Man now?" John paused thoughtfully. "Say he's gotta be someplace doing something wonderful, don't ya think?"

"I shore am," came an echoey voice from off in the distance.

"What did you say, Terry?"

"I didn't say anything."

"Oh, I thought for a minute...never mind. Let's step outside. I bet we got a dune buggy waiting for us!"

There it was. A shiny new dune buggy with bright yellow sides and orange flames painted on the panels. John thought it looked like the buggy of his dreams, the one he never got but always wanted. He thought he may have built a model of it once when he was a kid. There seemed to be no one around. In fact, they weren't even inside the mining compound anymore. It was just them, the high desert with its rolling foothills, and the mountain range to the west which John now clearly knew to be the Chuskas.

"OK, Terry. You drive."

Terry jumped with excitement like he was a kid again and shouted as he piled into the driver's seat. "Whoo hoo! I feel like the Old Man and a kid!"

Terry peeled out leaving a cloud of dust and they headed west toward the Chuska Mountains.

Chapter Two: Sadoval's Transition

"A few more miles should do it!" Terry shouted over the roaring engine. "Hey, I just had a *Deja vu!*"

"Rage a who?!" John shouted back hardly able to hear himself over the dune buggy's grinding and shifting. "You know you're supposed to shake the milk *before* you drink it!"

"What trinket!?" And the buggy came to an abrupt halt against a rock.

"Geez, now I'm really having a *Deja vu.*" Terry turned off the engine and jumped out. "I bet we broke the axle."

"How would you know that? You don't know anything about cars."

"Well, I been through this once before. You see those high-tension towers we've been following. They go right across the mountain top and down the west side. Broken Wing and I came up the other side about forty or fifty years from now and found the cabin. 'Course, I was havin' one heck of a withdrawal then." Terry smiled. "It sure is amazing how the universe comes back around on itself like that." Terry paused. "Ain't it Johnny?"

"Okay, okay. We're supposed to walk now, anyway. I could feel it just before you cracked up the dune buggy of my dreams."

"You know it doesn't make any difference, John."

"Yeah, I know. But I feel this longing inside and it kind of mixes up my emotions a bit. I think it's getting close to the time for me to be getting back to Jude and Sarah," John sighed. He no longer felt shame, he felt a compassionate desire to go to them and make amends, and, if Jude would have him, put forth his best effort to be a good father and husband. With the alcohol addiction removed, he was sure there would be some way to make good out of the mess he had created. He knew in his heart how capable he was of creating disasters. But now, new power seemed to have taken over his life, power that could make all things good. All he had to do was let go and let this new force be the motivating factor in all his affairs. He had let down a lot of people: his wife, daughter, co-workers, friends. He couldn't change what was already done, but he sure was willing to make amends for it. He felt willing and ready to go back and throw himself on their mercy, taking whatever fate had in store for him.

"I've got to go back, Terry."

"Soon, very soon," Terry said wisely, and they walked on in silence.

"And I've got to write a book!" John said abruptly.

"Yeah, I know. Ain't it grand!"

"I used to hate writing. That's why I wrote songs and poetry. Much shorter, more succinct. I was lazier then. I started writing at least twenty books. A few turned into short stories but the 'would be' books only went to two or three chapters. Some were fiction. Some non-fiction. But the funny thing is, even though I didn't really finish anything I started, it was all practice for the day when I would..."

"What day would that be, John. Tomorrow?"

"Yeah. I know. I can't write a book tomorrow. Now is the only time we can do anything. Tomorrow doesn't exist. That's it! That's what I'll write about. The motherlode exists only here and now! Not in the future. Not in the past. The discovery of all those things we think we need like good health, wealth, love, infinite supply. Everyone's looking for it, but they can't find it. Why? Because it's all in a secret place where almost no one ever looks:"

"The present moment!" they both exclaimed.

"I'm gonna sing Step by Step again- hey, wait! Look over there!"

"That's my cabin, John. Where Sadoval's been hanging out since the cavalry days. Where me and Broken Wing slid into our new lives. It's a cabin out of time. I bet it looked the same in 1845 as it does now and did fifty years from now...you know, John, I've been thinking this cabin doesn't have any sense of time. You know, like it exists somewhere outside of any timeline and it's here for any that are ready to live now in their new purpose." He looked far off into the sky. "It no longer seems to matter to me what time period I'm in."

"Now that's the Terry I always believed in, insightful, brilliant"

"Ya-te-hey!" interrupted Terry and John noticed Sadoval had appeared in the doorway and was waving them in.

"Come on, you two clowns. Stop all that fool-speak and come and eat," and they entered the magic cabin.

It had one large room with a kitchen area and large wood burning stove, a door to another room, probably the bedroom, John thought. Inside the back door was a pile of chopped firewood. He thought of it as a magic cabin not just because of what Terry said, but because the table was set for three and loaded with everyone's favorite food, because Sadoval must be almost 140 years old, because it seemed to appear out of nowhere like a Lilliputian Island and because he would have expected only juniper berries and corn to eat way up here. But no! It was a feast!

The three men embraced silently and dove into the meal. Sadoval was eating frybread, corn, some kind of green leafy vegetable and beans. John's food was Chinese chicken fried rice, his all-time favorite. Terry's plate was piled with little mini steak sandwiches. 'Steakies' he used to call them. John remembered eating them for lunch when they were kids on one of those rare days when they went to Terry's house to play, probably when Terry's Dad was on a hunting trip. Terry told him then that he loved those little steakies. John thought a little music would be nice, they were such noisy eaters, and an old song by some seventies rock star he couldn't remember began playing from out of nowhere, something about loving your pants.

After dinner they sat on the porch. John felt satisfied and at peace with his two friends. It was as if they had always been together. They were on the western slope of one of the Chuska Mountains, high enough to be in rain country where tall grass and trees formed a lush green savannah. The cabin was on a rock outcropping so that it afforded a view for miles to the west. John thought he could see high desert country off in the distance where an orange sunset was setting the rocks on fire with its brilliance. Sadoval spoke first.

"Five years ago, you sent me up here to pray the Medicine Way for my people, five years that have seemed like only a day."

"Well it's been only a day for us," John interjected, and Terry hushed him with a look that said, 'This is Sadoval's time. Let him speak.' John could feel his chest tingling with excitement.

"Hmmm. Still not sure how that works..." Sadoval paused. "It has been a glorious time for me. I have felt more peace than I have ever known. My heart has become so light, I sometimes feel it will lead me into the air. I know the souls of my people are safe, but their lives at this time are headed into many hardships because of the mines. I see that, but I see something else. A new way that is an old way. The way the ancestors speak of when I call upon them. A way of infinite wisdom. When I studied English, I spent much time thinking about this word, 'infinite'. I began to get visions of how to live life here on our Mother Earth. I don't mean visions of the details of what jobs I would work, what relations I would have or other worldly pursuits. I mean visions of a whole new way to live. One vision came to me in a dream last night.

"There was a tower, like the silos you find on the farms up north where you men come from. The silo was made of wood on a brick and mortar foundation. In my dream, the wood was rotten and gray with many holes and the roof on top was mostly collapsed. I looked closer and saw that some of the bricks had been removed going toward the left side. The faded old bricks were scattered on the ground as if the silo were undergoing some kind of reconstruction. Right in front, where the first bricks had been removed, a few new bricks had been mortared in to the height of the old foundation. They had been taken from a pallet of bricks sitting to the right of the silo. The new bricks were a shiny silver that sparkled in the sunlight. Above the silver bricks that had been placed in the foundation, as if coming from them, a silver line as wide as one of the bricks was seeping its silvery glow upward into the decayed silo wood. The silver strip worked its way to the top of the silo. Wherever it touched, it rebuilt the wall of the silo turning old gray rotted wood into this new shiny silver. When the silver streak reached the top of the old round roof, it formed a silver needle that stuck way up into the sky. The top of the needle was sending forth a silvery glow in all directions like it was broadcasting it over the whole Earth. I wept tears of overwhelming joy as I realized the silver glow was pure love, so full and complete that it provided for everyone in the most beautiful way. Me, my people, all people on Earth were being restored like the silo from a new foundation.

"A new way that is the old way. The oldest way of all time. The way of infinite wisdom, infinite love. The ancestors always represented infinite wisdom for me. Now I know it is Infinity itself that I belong to, that everyone belongs to. And when anyone is ready to let go of their human self, their ego, their own ambitions, they will see this new foundation being built for them, brick by brick, piece by piece, giving them a new foundation from which to make their choices. Choices not based on greed and lust, fear and poverty, opinions and judgements, hopes and desires, fear of evil and love of good. But choices based on this new foundation more precious than silver or gold that is the substance of all being. 'Let go. Let go. Let go of all our human ways', it says. This new foundation is the cause that will produce the effect of changing lives into something more wonderful than anything we could imagine or do from the limitations of mind."

The tingling in John's chest had moved into his entire body. There was a shimmering silver glow all around him. Terry was glowing too and laughing out loud. Sadoval lifted his arms and opened his palms toward the sky. The shimmering silver flow of energy was coming through all of them and seemed to have no beginning and no end. John could see the silhouette of a man ascending from under the Earth. He was dressed from head to toe in white buckskin with long flowing fringe dangling from the arms and down the legs. He floated up and came to rest in front of Sadoval. His eyes were emitting colorful sparks and he was wearing a headdress of feathers that went down his back to the ground and glowed with all the colors of the rainbow. Each feather would constantly change colors, red, orange, yellow, green, blue, indigo and violet, giving a pulsating impression. It was the most glorious display of lights John had ever seen.

"I am you and you are me," the apparition said in a quiet voice that seemed to come from inside John's head.

"I am the friend you have sought," the voice continued from inside and out. "I am with you always giving you everything. Beyond dreams and hopes, beyond desires, beyond all pain and sorrow, I give constantly everything you need for you and the lives you touch. I am your one true friend, the one

you can always count on, for I am with you always. *I am you.*"

The figure took Sadoval's hands. John saw Terry standing up to join them. John stood and joined them. Everyone's hands were joined and lifted above their heads, but it was as if everyone was reaching to everyone else and it was impossible to see who had started it. He looked at Terry and knew Terry could see it as well. There was no difference between any of them. They were all one in a glowing, shimmering colorful globe of energy that was expanding to cover the Earth and sky. The heavens were singing in a thousand voice chorus to a thousand-piece orchestra coming from all directions at once. The words were unintelligible yet loud and clear. They made no sense yet seemed to convey all knowledge ever known. John was fully awakened and aware that he, his friends, and all people had a place and a purpose. He cried out in laughter and tears unable to hold in the joy lest he should burst into flames. He had never known such unity and fulness before, yet he felt as if he had always known, known that he, John, an individual speck of sand among countless specks, was just as important, just as loved, just as capable of loving and just as precious as all the other specks. In that moment he knew that this is what makes us one and a part of this universal wonder.

In the blink of an eye, with no fanfare or explosion of lights, Sadoval and the buckskinned apparition were gone, and John stood next to Terry in the quiet, watching the stars appear like pinholes in a dark blue canopy. They remained there until the sky turned ink black and was alive with constellations brighter and more beautiful than John had ever seen.

Chapter Three: John's Light

"Today is the tomorrow I worried about yesterday. That is the old way. The new way is, express love, peace and harmony now and tomorrow will take care of itself in ways better than you can imagine..."

"Hmm... how's that sound, Terry. You think I got it right?" queried John.

"I wouldn't know. Not my field," said Terry nonchalantly as he sat back in the large straw chair on the cabin porch toothpick in hand picking celery strings out of his teeth from the big lunch they had just eaten.

"Oh, yeah, I forgot. You're not my guru, I am."

"Yes, how quickly we can forget."

"Well, I have to keep writing. It still feels a little weird not having an agent, a publisher, or even a plan for the future of this thing. I'm still not sure if it's a story, an article, a novel or what. I don't even know my target audience. It is really cool, though, getting quiet, listening to the silence, getting that joyful fulfilling feeling, then writing. Being on this mountain really seems to help. And I always feel so happy after I finish a section. Like I want to dance with the Old Man again. Never thought I was a dancer, though."

"Yeah, you got that sense of satisfaction because you're in your element now. You're doing what you're meant to do. I get that from waiting. Waiting is my purpose right now. Who said nothing is impossible? I'm doing nothing right now, heh heh." Terry laughed like the Old Man.

"In a moment of love, we lose all sense of having to do something, know something, or understand something. We are not disturbed or affected by anything."

"This is so easy to write, probably because I've experienced all those things. It's not theory or philosophy. It's experience. I like it!"

"And I like your music, John. You got another song?"

"You know if I start singing, we never know what's going to happen. Every time I sing it's like 'Step by Step' and we could end up God knows where. I'll sing if it hits me. Right now I've got to write. So writing it is!"

"Today is that day of translation for us. 'Transition,' pardon me. This is the day we make the decision to forget those

things that are behind and to reach for those things which are, um...a...those things which are in front of us.   A transformation of your life is in progress," John read. "It's been great to see so many transformations. William, Hector, Sadoval..."

"Yes, and Broken Wing," interjected Terry. "He would dazzle you if you met him. He was always an amazing friend to me, but, boy, what amazing things he must be doing now with his people."

"We lose all sense of having to do something, know something, or understand something.   Hmmm... I like that but maybe it's out of sequence," pondered John.

"To know everything is to know nothing. To know nothing is to know everything. Hey, you should write *that* one down, Johnny!" Terry mimicked the Old Man.

"I used to think peace and contentment would mean a boring life. No ups and downs. No turns in the road. Just smooth sailing, no excitement. Boy was I wrong. I never know what's going to turn up next. And I'm never surprised, but always excited. I always seem to have at hand what it takes to handle every new situation.   And you.   You're so amazingly clever. The brain, your sister used to call you when we were kids."

"One who has devoted time to meditation is not bewildered when the experience comes, with practice it can be attained at will," Terry beamed. "There's another one for ya'."

"OK. OK. Read this for a while." John threw an old newspaper at Terry. "Maybe Prince Valiant got a new girlfriend." They both laughed.

"Hey, Terry?"

"Yeah?"

"Does everything always make sense to you?"

"What I sense with my senses makes sense in a sensory sense."

"Naw, come on. I'm serious. Do you get everything?"

"Well, what I get is a constant endless supply of everything needed for every given moment."

"Yes, I-I know that now, too. We get it, not because we do the right thing, or behave a certain way, or ask in the right manner. We get it because it is our birthright as human beings. It is everyone's birthright."

"It is, but I didn't see it or take advantage of it un-until I came to such a point that my ego and my entire sense of well-being, what little of it I had, collapsed into a pile of shit and I lay there in my own stink."

"And buried in the midst of that pile of shit was a bright, beautiful pony-"quipped John.

"Yeah, yeah, but it is so much more than that. You see, I burned all my bridges and left no one behind. When I turn myself in to the authorities back home, I will have to make the final step in atonement. I don't know what will happen, but still, I will go in spite of any worries or fears."

"Yeah, Terry, I'm not worried about myself any more either. Living by fear? It's gone. Loneliness? Depression? Things of the past..." John paused and saw his entire life flash before him. His emotions no longer told him he was lower than worm slime because of his past deeds, for he understood completely that the past cannot be changed. Even with the Old Man, Terry's peace-making hand gestures and John's step by step magic, they never changed the past. They only observed it and shared what they had with everyone they met. Now John's focus was on others and how he could contribute to life. This new found power that seemed to surge through him could do that. And he trusted that it would.

"But, what about Judith and Sarah?" John said and his eyes filled with tears. He had to pause a moment to collect himself. "I-I still feel like I should go back there and change the past. Not all of it, just the evening that ended up with her leaving. I can see myself so clearly driving home that evening, smashing Sarah's tricycle, yelling at that sweet innocent little girl, getting drunk and finding out the next day that I had created the ultimate disaster. And I still don't know what I did! If only I could go back and..."

"Thar ya go, Johnny. Ya' got it right!" John and Terry looked at the open back door of the cabin and saw the silhouette of a man in a corny tattered straw hat.

"Old Man!" they said in tandem.

"Yep. Ya got it right."

"What did I get right?" asked John.

"It's in the driveway, Johnny. The driveway!" the Old Man chuckled.

"What do you mean?" said John.

"Think about it fer a minute. What was going on in yer head when you pulled into the driveway that night and almost hit yer daughter's trike?" the Old Man asked.

"Well, I was nervous and felt really shaky. I'd been working all day and couldn't wait to get home. Not to see Jude and Sarah," with that more tears came, and he sobbed, "but-but to get to that bottle of brandy."

"Yup. That's the illusion, ain't it?"

"The illusion, of course! The illusion that the bottle was my only friend. That I couldn't live without it. I couldn't wait to get home to it. It gave me temporary comfort, friendship, companionship, freedom from fear, emotional pain, the works!" John paused. Terry and the Old Man looked on in silence. John continued.

"Ah, but the illusion is that the bottle did actually give me all those things. The reality is it gave me nothing. Nothing at all. My fears, pain, loneliness, despair and confusion were not eliminated by alcohol. They kept on and grew because I did not face them. I did not look inside myself. I was too scared to look inside. All I knew to do was look to things on the outside that would make me feel good - people, jobs, relationships, alcohol. In fact, I wasn't just using alcohol, I was using people trying to fill the emptiness inside. That emptiness seemed real, but it wasn't. Cause now I've looked past it and found the motherlode. I've got so much; it's overflowing and all I want to do is give out to others."

"You found it, just like me," said Terry.

"But I found it too late, didn't I?

"Remember, John," the Old Man said in his serious voice, "time is not what you think it is. Your life is what you make it. It is your consciousness that brings forth the people and events in your life and since that last evening with your family, how much time has passed?"

"Why, I don't even know."

"John..." Terry paused. "You know, John, I have to go take care of things back home," said Terry, "and I don't know how long it'll take, but the time in which everything real and important is happening is now. This time is for you. Your conscious life since you woke up in the desert with a hangover has been involved in revelation after revelation. You have made a beginning in sharing those revelations with others, who are now making new choices based on their own revelation of the infinite good they had always possessed. That is the hope of mankind. In the meantime, your wife and child have not been a part of your life, yet they have remained in your heart, and that is the real part. "

"W-what is?" asked John.

"Love. The real part is love," continued Terry. "When you realize that, you begin to realize you are an expression of love. You are the only one who can express and experience love for you. As you express it, love seems to be triggered in others and they also start to express it."

"I wish to express love to my family- " John began.

"Love is an expression now, in this moment. Start here and now. Don't wait until you see the right people or find the right time 'because it'll never come. The right time and the only time is now. Express it now and amazing things will transpire in ways better than you could ever imagine," Terry concluded.

"And furthermore," said the Old Man in his most serious voice, "you can't outline how and where love shall go or to whom it will be given. Why not, you may ask? Well I'll tell you-"

The Old Man stood up tall and straight and looked, to John like he had become a giant and his voice echoed across the mountains.

"You have been waiting and wanting to give love all your life. Now you are ready. You have stepped out of time, away from your family, to find out who you are and the true meaning of love. This has been like a dream and you are about to wake up. Except these adventures with us really happened, and yet they no longer exist because they are now in the past. Right now, you are ready and willing to go back and do the next right thing. And go back you must, to the moment you stepped out of time. The moment that started you on your last drunk."

"I just made a decision! shouted John. "I am choosing the other side. I can see clearly now exactly who I am and what I am made of...it *is* love. Always has been. And now I can see it in everyone I meet! I've got to go back!"

"Oh boy, Johnny, ya' did it now. Ya' put yerself in the hands of fate. Ya' ain't got no idea what's 'a' gonna happen next, " the Old Man said with a sparkle in his eyes.

"Ooh I want so much to make things right!" John exclaimed.

"You ain't got the power, Johnny. Things are right already. Jes' let 'em happen."

"Can you see it now, John?" asked Terry. "Turning into the driveway is the turning point in your life. You turned into it the first time in alcoholic desperation, in fear and illusion, your mind spinning with a thousand thoughts based on guilt, shame and that ugly feeling you carried with you that you were lower than worm-slime and didn't even have a right to breath air. The mysterious voice from behind the furnace was there calling you to wake up, but you couldn't understand it."

Terry then held his palms upward in front of him and John saw something like a ball of light forming above them. "They are still there, John, waiting. Waiting for you to come home with open arms. They have not yet experienced the painful disaster that was implied in the note you read that next morning. But I can guarantee you that a disaster was bound to happen if you didn't wake up. What went on from that evening to this moment was entirely for your own personal transformation. You have been chosen, by your own heart, to live out your life as love. You have realized the power to turn everything around. You can go back."

"So-so all of time and eternity has been put on hold just for me?" asked John.

"No, just your time and your loved ones. Everyone has a turning point. Your turning point came in the driveway. You had to experience the rest in order to be free. Now you are free, and you can continue, still the same John, social worker, musician, husband and father, but with a new foundation of trust in what is inside you. And with a few surprising differences, Mr. John Whitlock, author, composer and gentleman!"

"But you and the Old Man, you're my friends!" John took a deep breath and remembered his new truth. "And you always will be as our hearts are united as Love. For we have all found, in our lives, that one lone friend that is the Friend to all, in all, and a part of all. We are that Friend and we all walk together. And we shall see humanity awaken, one by one, to this new foundation of love and trust, of the endless supply of all things good. *It is so beautiful.*"

John's eyes were filled with tears and his smile was so spontaneous and bright that it shimmered forth from his face. The brightness expanded and joined with the ball of light above Terry's palms. John saw Terry surrounded by an aura of light that grew and blended with his and the Old Man's. Their bodies, the cabin and the shapes of the furniture faded into the light. John felt a lightness like he had never felt before. This was not the lightness he felt when he was relieved of his pain and guilt. This was not the shedding of a horrible past. This was the light that knows no darkness. The Light that is the very essence of all things. He felt at one with everyone and everything. He felt the beautiful presence in this precious present moment which seemed to encompass all time.

Space and time blended into the one great light as everything became light, and all darkness was gone.

John closed his eyes, took a deep breath, and stepped forward.

Chapter Four: The Return

John drove his car carefully into his driveway and stopped, just avoiding hitting the tricycle with his gray Chevy Cavalier. *Sweet, dear Sarah. she must be out here playing somewhere.* Sarah came around from the side of the house with arms outstretched.

"Daddy, Daddy!" she cried out.

John scooped her up in his arms and gave her a great big hug. "Oh, Sarah how wonderful you are. It is so good to see you!" He gave her multiple cheek kisses and she giggled, "Aww, Daddy, 'top it, 'top it!" She giggled some more, and he carried her toward the house bouncing all the way.

Judith was standing in the doorway watching with a quizzical look on her face. "John? Are you all right?"

"Judith!" He put Sarah down inside the door and reached out to his wife and gave her a long deep hug. He looked over her shoulder into the house, knowing full well he had only left it this morning as far as she was concerned, but realizing in his heart that this was his new home, the home his loving heart always knew was possible, the home he could now live.

"Why, John..." John could feel Judith's body going from tense to relaxed as they held each other. It felt like the first time they had ever hugged, warm, soft, sweet and safe in each other's' arms.

He held Judith at arm's length and looked deeply into her eyes. Yes, this was the lightest of all feelings he had ever experienced. Lighter than when he had shed past burdens in the desert with the Old Man. Lighter than when his soul seemed to soar above the mountains. Lighter than the experience at Sadoval's transition. So light he could not keep still. He began to sway with Judith in his arms. They swayed together as it built into a dance. They moved around the room with ballroom grace and Sarah giggled with delight and danced in circles with them. They danced to silent music that seemed to crescendo in John's head. Judith smiled as big and bright as she had on their wedding day. They joined hands laughing and dancing in a circle around the room. It was happiness long suppressed, now alive and freely expressed. They were speechless as they finished their dance and plopped on the living room carpet, gazing into each other's eyes with love and trust.

Sarah snuggled in the crook of her Daddy's arm and smiled up at him. It felt so good to be so close again. Doubt flashed through John's mind for a moment that he did not deserve all this. He quickly remembered it was his birthright, and he only need accept it and surrender to it completely and he would be assured that this was real. Through her smile, Judith looked at him quizzically and cautiously asked, "Did something happen at work today?" She stiffened up a little waiting for a reply.

"Jude, you are, now, and always have been my soulmate, lover and friend." John paused and noticed Judith relaxing a bit. "All the love that you've given me, the honesty, you have been more than good to this family. You've been like an angel. It is me that's fallen short. I have not been there for you when I should, I have not given my whole heart's attention at home... with you, and Sarah. My drinking had me bound in self-centered selfish behavior and that is entirely my fault.

"But it isn't words or empty apologies I want to give you. I desire only the chance to show my love to you and be the man we both know I can be, as long as I stay sober and practice my program. So...Judith, will you be my wife and take me as your husband, so we can work together to build a new life, a life of peace, love and harmony and help make a better world?"

"John...are you going to stop drinking and get back into AA?"

John was stupefied. Being so wrapped up in his own revelations, he wasn't thinking of Judith at all. *First things first,* said a familiar voice in his head. Not taking the first drink was first and he needed to put his priorities in order. To Judith, this would be his first day sober, and, as far as she knew, he was planning to get drunk right now. This thought humbled him, bringing him to the reality that he had a lot of amends to make. "Of course...of course, my love. That is where my friends are, my life, my sobriety, so much more."

"John, when we started out, I did not know you as a drinker. You had your AA program and friends and I could see and feel that wonderful spirit that was in you, that led you. After Sarah was born, you drank again. That made no sense to me, and it changed you, John, changed you... into something I did not understand at all. It just didn't fit with the 'you' I had fallen in love with. The beautiful home we had begun to build was beginning to fall apart. I was afraid. When you were sober before, I didn't have to deal with a lot of my fears. In fact, I didn't even know I had some of them. But I came to realize fear is the motivating force behind alcoholism and our whole family is affected."

Judith paused and, in a moment of clarity, John confessed, "I-I really thought my true nature was dark, evil, destructive. And my drinking and... and... all the *things* I did seemed to prove it." His admission to Judith came out in an uncontrollable sob.

Judith responded firmly, "John, I know. I know all about the other woman. I know what you were doing. I'm not blind. Al-Anon has taught me that much. But I also know you have a disease, a disease that can only be cured by a spiritual experience. I've been waiting, knowing in my heart it would come. The spirit that was in you when we met...it would show itself again." She paused for a second and took a deep breath. "And, almost beyond hope, I can sense something different in you right now."

John spoke again, slowly at first, then picking up the pace as if someone else was doing the talking for him. "All along the truth had been inside me, buried underneath my fears and self-hatred. The truth has been with me my entire life, sometimes haunting me, sometimes disturbing me, but always available to give me strength if I would just be willing to let it. It was around when I was a lost child, scared, in the basement. It was there for me all through my drinking waiting for me to become willing to trust in it, and I am certain now it is around forever." He paused again and looked off into the distance contemplating the new realm he had stepped into with Terry and the Old Man.

Judith's eyes seemed to go past John, like she was focusing on something far beyond the room. Her silent gaze told him she was listening intently and waiting for more. Or was she resting in the same peace that he was feeling? He could feel his heart, filled with joy, beating in rhythm with hers. He saw the familiar column of sparkling silver-gray energy flowing back and forth between them, moving in a stream up and down from the sky, expanding out and turning brighter and brighter as it moved over little Sarah. The three stood as one in this shimmering light. Now the connection went beyond marriage and family. It was all love, for all, in all, of all and above all. He was more grateful than he had ever thought he could be.

"Do you see it, Jude? Do you see what I see? It's a pure force that covers us all! It's so-o-o-o real!"

"Yes, I see it John. I have seen it for some time now. And now we see it together! Even Sarah can. Look at her!"

And Sarah was standing tall and still bathed in pure white light. As John watched, her figure seemed to transform several times in succession. He saw dozens, maybe hundreds and thousands of faces of children of all races. Then, she was a small Navajo girl, then a mother with a child in her arms, then the light became so bright he couldn't see her at all, but only heard her laughter.

"I see it in Sarah's face!" He gave Sarah a squeeze, and, although the light seemed to be gone, what was left was the feeling of the light which John could only call love, peace and harmony. "It's here in every hug, in every caring gesture we make to each other, to others. When we help someone else, when we share a good word. It's always been here, and I've been blind to it." John turned to Judith and softly said, "Jude, I don't expect your forgiveness for my drinking. I simply ask you, give me, give us... a new chance."

What Judith said next surprised John, but, at the same time, seemed like the most natural and normal thing he could hear.

"Oh, John...Johnny...Johnny, yes, I like the sound of that. Johnny! Hey, Sarah, I called Daddy, Johnny. Isn't that funny?" She pursed her lips into her cute face. "Yes, its so funny." She tickled Sarah and they both went into a giggle fit. John laughed, too. Their combined laughter seemed to meld into one voice, a voice that shouted without words. A voice that was happy, joyous and free!

After a few moments, they calmed down and Judith said, "Hey, we've got dinner to make. I've been at Day Care all afternoon. Today was Mother's Day Out, you know, and it was my turn to watch the kids."

"Let's order a pizza!" John exclaimed.

"Peetza! Peetza! Peetza!" was Sarah's knowing reply.

"Aah, we can make one ourselves a lot better," Judith said firmly. "Come on, kids, into the kitchen we go!"

Sarah and Judith ran into the kitchen. John stood up slowly, amazed and grateful at how this was working out. *It probably will always amaze me,* he thought. *And all I have to do is show up, believe it, live it, share it. It's all so simple. How could I have ever missed it before? So simple, so simple...*

At that moment, John heard the roaring of an engine out front. "Just a minute, Jude, I think someone pulled in the driveway."

He went to the screen door and saw that bright yellow dune buggy of his dreams with orange flames on the side. And there behind the wheel was Terry, smiling and waving.

"I thought you had places to go, buddy," said John as he walked up to the buggy.

"Yup. It's all taken care of. Seems those days we were together were for me, too, and I get to begin my life wherever I choose. I think I may just stay in Austin for a while. Whaddaya say, Johnny!"

"Come on in, old man. We're makin' pizza."

Postlude:
The Guides II

It was Saturday morning and John Whitlock was cheerfully sweeping out the garage of his modest suburban Austin ranch home. He thought about this last year with Sarah and Judith. He had not only abstained from alcohol; he had completely lost the desire to drink. Being sober kept him alert and aware. With a clear mind, he could practice realizing and expressing the presence of love all day long. In this period of reconstruction of his home, work and social life, he found that most people were forgiving and that he had been viewed more as a troubled alcoholic than as a bad person. Regaining trust in his relationships took time, but he approached it with the patience that came from practicing gratitude and trusting the love he had discovered within himself. He would take a few moments several times a day to quiet his mind and connect with that realization. All situations he encountered worked out in ways that were of benefit to all concerned, including adversarial relationships. On this new basis, he made his decisions based on trust, not fear.

Working a program of sobriety meant putting concern for others first. He was no longer obsessed with himself, his selfish needs and his personal fulfillment. He found happiness in helping others. He kept his social work job because it afforded ample opportunity to give what he had been so graciously given. He reached out to other alcoholics who were still struggling and shared his experience and new found strength with them. He finished his first writing, which turned out to be a novel first published as an audiobook, complete with music and songs he had written to go with the story.

But most of all, he had learned the true meaning of love with his wife and daughter. Accepting and receiving love among them had become an easy, normal way of life. And, as a family, they expressed this to others and the effects of their love spread to many.

John understood that he was born to express love, goodness, kindness and so much more, that these were gifts given to him to give away to others. He took no credit for them. He wrote in his book that he saw himself like a river letting the waters flow out to fill the sea. Love is the water, and the sea is all of humanity. The spirit of humility had taken over. In the last year, his loved ones and colleagues saw and accepted the change in John and trusted it, and many of them changed as well.

He thought of all of his new adventures with Terry since Terry moved to Austin. The Old Man had been right. The battles were always won with make-believe swords against enemies that seemed real at first but became fantasy and disappeared into nothingness. No one was hurt and everyone won. They showed up together in many places meeting many people and it was always the same. People changed. Lives changed. Before their very eyes, lives were transformed with what seemed like no effort on their part. John just put one foot forward and they showed up right where they belonged, at the exact moment their presence was needed. With a wave of the hand, Terry sent out love, peace and harmony. But John knew it wasn't them doing something to the other person. It was the other person who was ready to change and discover and live their lives on a new foundation, the shining, shimmering silvery foundation that rebuilt their lives into something more amazing than they ever could have imagined.

There were the newly sober alcoholics John met often in AA, and the drug addicts Terry saw in the jails. Yes, it was amazing that Terry was visiting jails. Facing his past, he had come clean to his old partner and the authorities and they let him off, which by all accounts should not have happened. Some called it a miracle. Terry and John knew the truth. It left Terry free to help other addicts and dealers. What the world called miracles, John knew as the realization of our true legacy and the love that flows from inside the person, out to the world.

John stopped sweeping the floor and stood in the dusty dimness of the garage leaning on the broom. He pondered the millions of dust particles aroused from their week long slumber by his broom, turned into shimmering diamonds in the sunbeam shining through the window above the garage door. He stood still and watched the tiny silvery sparkles swirl in the sunlight and disappear beyond its borders. He glanced over at his single furnace and remembered the three furnaces in the triplex he lived in as a child. They had been lined up near the back wall and they loomed in the silence like dependable steady thoughts waiting quietly to be brought forth to dissolve the cacophony of fears and worries that had been so familiar to him then.

John took time to feel the silence and quiet his mind. That familiar sensation of safety and comfort welled up in his chest. His childhood memory was so vivid that the three furnaces seemed to materialize in the gray shadows and emit a silvery glow. The glow seemed even more real as he watched the ghost furnaces transform into three human-like figures almost indistinguishable in the dimness.

The figure on the left stepped into the shimmering sunbeam and John saw that it was Sadoval. He impulsively started to step forward but Sadoval lifted his hand and bade him stop. The middle figure stepped forward into the sunlight. It was the Old Man! John had not seen him in over a year and his heart leaped with joy. They all stood motionless, speechless, sharing the sanctity of the moment and relishing the abundance of love now present, now realized, now flooding the garage with its Divine aura.

John spoke without thinking. "You have been with me all along, since the tormented days of my youth, guiding me, helping me, when I could not help myself. You are truly Masters and I am filled with overwhelming gratitude for all you have done." The words came out of their own accord. It was not him speaking and yet it was him.

John closed his eyes and shook his head. When he opened them, the figures were still present, smiling, standing in the silent stillness. "But why are you here? I have no need of you now. I have been endowed with the legacy of love and trust and am now able to help others. You must have more important work to do? Others to help?"

Sadoval and the Old Man slowly motioned to their left drawing John's attention to the third figure standing just out of the light of the sunbeam. The blurry figure disappeared behind the one lone garage furnace. The Old Man laughed. John's heart jumped with fear and excitement. He moved quickly to the furnace and peeked behind it. He saw nothing as his heart pounded against his ears. He walked all the way around it and, seeing nothing, darted back the other way. The Old Man and Sadoval were both laughing now as John kept running back and forth around the furnace trying to catch a glimpse of the blurry figure. The more he ran around, the more he was determined to catch this guy. He was positive this was the one he thought he saw as a kid in that basement long ago. He really wanted to know who it was. It was all consuming. He had to know.

He ran as fast as he could in one direction, around and around. He must have circled the furnace a dozen times by now. The laughter was uproarious. John was out of breath. He finally stopped and leaned against the basement wall.

"Ya know, if', ya' go fast enuf, ya' might catch yerself," the Old Man said between guffaws.

"Man who chase himself is like cat chasing tail," added Sadoval in a wise old Indian voice.

"Oh, shit!" John shouted. "It was me! It was me all along! I was the one saving me: in the basement, in the swamp, in all my adventures. It was always me! I never believed I had it in me! But it was me all along! I just couldn't see it. It was never you guys at all!" John was incredulous as he beamed with this new awakening.

"Yep, Johnny. It was you 'n me 'n Sadoval 'n Terry 'n all those other folks workin' together." The Old Man's voice changed. "But ultimately, the source of power to lead one's own destiny must be found by the individual inside his own being. That is where it always is, for each person is born with this very thing. It is the ability to sustain one's self. Yet it is far more than self-sufficiency. Once discovered, a great humility overcomes the person as he realizes it is a gift to him, and he is overwhelmed with the pouring out of this love as he connects with others through love, not hate, jealousy, anger, envy and the like. And because of this, he can then realize we are all one in a spirit of trust. Then it no longer matters who is doing what for whom because it all comes from the same source, the infinite source of love. The discovery of this is what leads to healing of illnesses, changing war into peace, sadness to joy and discord to harmony."

Sadoval took over. "When I was praying the Medicine Way for my people, after over one hundred years, I awakened. I realized the Medicine Way was not to heal my people from the illnesses and destruction caused by the uranium mining. It was not to heal the white man of his greed and lust for power. Of course, at first, I thought it was for all that. It was a noble gesture on my part, though somewhat judgmental toward the white man. But the more I prayed, the more I listened until, finally, I stopped using my ceremonies and gestures for asking for anything. I began to listen instead. Only listen. As I listened, I awakened to what was inside me. The inner silver glow of life that made up my true self. I was not this body. I was not this mind. I was this silver glow that I found residing deep within myself. This is the true self. As I realized this, I realized everyone has their own true self inside. The body is simply its home. I had been judging people by their appearances, their actions, their beliefs. I had been seeing only their shell, not the inner soul that is the source."

Sadoval paused and the Old Man added, "It is presumptuous for us to think we know what is best for others. Whether we are religious or not, we often pray to whatever we believe to fix things the way we think they should be fixed. To heal people the way we think they should be healed. To change people from what we think is bad to what we think is good. We are supported in this effort by the people around us who agree on what is right and what is wrong. It is a reasonable way of thinking. But it is ineffective. Churches are filled with people praying daily for wars to end and sick children to get well, yet the prayers go mostly unanswered. So many are praying so earnestly. But who are they praying too? Many say they are praying to a loving god who always takes care of his people. Wouldn't a loving God take care of his creations always? Would a loving God create suffering, or let suffering happen to his creations just because they did not ask him for help correctly? Would that really be love. It is like this god is saying, 'I will grant your wishes, but only if you ask me correctly,' or in some right way that is often difficult to understand."

"Yes," said John. "'It's already here', you said to me once. I don't have to pray for anything to get better because it is already perfect. I just couldn't see it before. Finding solutions to the world's problems is only a temporary fix anyway, if it even works at all. Knowing, truly knowing, all is well and good leaves us with only one thing to do. Give it away. Give away this love and goodness! Give away peace, love and harmony! The more we give it out, the more we have it, and the more it affects everyone! And how I love giving it away! I love sharing my joy with newly sober alcoholics. Terry, too. And you loved sharing your joy with me, Old Man. And, boy, how you did share it when I discovered you in the desert in that crazy dune buggy!"

"Hee, hee. Ain't life a pip, Johnny!"

"Hey, you guys wanna stay for dinner!"

"Nope, it don't work that way no more, Johnny,' said the Old Man.

"We, each of us, step in our own way," added Sadoval.

"Yet we are always together, as one, our souls of light connected with shimmering silver columns of energy to the one light that envelopes all," John realized. "Hey, I've got to write that one down!"

"Yep, you go write another book. I'm a gonna get me a pretzel!"

And the Old Man, who never needed a name, and Sadoval, the timeless native Spirit, dissolved into a million shimmering silver sparks that blended into the sunbeam and followed it up and out the window. John's heart continued to be filled with a joy so great he would spend the rest of his life sharing it through writing, music and many other ways that would always come to him at the right time and in the right place.

And the more he shared, the lighter the world became.

Fine

Look for Book II of the Lopeha Adventures:

Rushing Waters

by Bill Webb

To be published late 2019

Go to:

www.billwebbmusic.com

for:

- The companion album, "One Lone Friend" to hear the music from the book,

- The Lopeha Adventure novel updates,

- All of Bill Webb's music/videos/podcasts,

- Native American Flute Music Podcasts,

- Dozens of peaceful music videos,

- The Bill Webb Blog

- Also, facebook.com/NativeAmericanFlute

- and...@billwebbmusic on Twitter

Love, Peace, Harmony in you,

now...

LOPEHA

www.ingramcontent.com/pod-product-compliance
Lightning Source LLC
Chambersburg PA
CBHW030330200626
46816CB00006BA/1994

* 9 7 8 1 7 3 2 9 3 9 6 1 5 *